For Mum x

CHAPTER 1

"HAVE YOU SEEN THIS, HARPER?" My sister, Jess, breathlessly rushed through the diner, before stopping in front of the table I was clearing and waving a brightly colored flyer in front of my face.

I plucked it from her fingertips and read:

The Yoga Goddess invites you to her new studio. The first lesson is free so what are you waiting for? Be prepared to get in touch with your inner goddess...

I pulled a face.

"There's a class tomorrow morning. I've signed us up," Jess announced proudly.

"I don't know," I said doubtfully as I scooped up two empty coffee cups. "I'm not sure I even have an inner goddess."

Jess pouted. "Come on, Harper. It will be fun."

The idea of turning my body into a human pretzel didn't sound like fun to me. It was all right for Jess. She was flexible.

My sister had inherited all the sporty genes. I'd inherited the genes that made me suited to sitting on the couch and reading books.

Jess loved trying out different types of exercise. She had been over the moon when a Pilates class started up in Abbott Cove last year. Unfortunately, Mrs. Tomlinson, who was eighty-three, had taken to the machines a little too enthusiastically. She'd snuck in the night before her class, intending to get a little practice, and ended up tangled in the machine, hanging upside down. She screamed for help until she was rescued by the fire service. The Pilates instructor had left Abbott Cove shortly afterward.

As Grandma Grant said, no one could accuse the residents of Abbott Cove of being unenthusiastic. Sometimes, they were a little too enthusiastic for their own good.

I caught sight of my boss, Archie waving at me frantically. We were a little short-staffed today.

I agreed to go with Jess just so I could get back to work before Archie popped a blood vessel. I mean, it was only yoga. How bad could it be? I should suggest the class to Archie. It was meant to be relaxing, and Archie could use a little relaxation. I liked my boss, but he was highly-strung. He referred to himself as a perfectionist, but I saw him more like a walking advert for high-blood pressure.

"I'll go, but I don't think the woman running the classes is going to be very popular."

"Why ever not?" Jess asked.

A WITCHY MYSTERY

HARPER GRANT MYSTERY SERIES BOOK TWO

DANICA BRITTON

"She has been in the diner a few times, and she is…" I searched for the right word but came up blank. "Difficult."

Difficult wasn't a strong enough word to describe Yvonne, in my opinion, but work wasn't a suitable place to say the other word that popped into my mind.

Jess frowned. "I think you have already made up your mind not to enjoy the class."

I rolled my eyes. "Wait until you meet her then you'll know what I mean. Are you staying for coffee?"

Jess shook her head. "I can't. I have to open the library. It's just me this morning."

I finished clearing the table as my sister left the diner as swiftly as she'd arrived.

My hands piled high with a stack of plates, I turned and walked straight through Loretta. I shivered.

"Well, that was rude," she said, folding her arms over her chest.

"Sorry, I muttered. I didn't see you there." I kept my voice down. The last thing I wanted was for the people in the diner to think I was talking to thin air.

I should probably explain in case you think I'm a nutcase. My name is Harper Grant, and I'm a witch. My particular talent is seeing ghosts and communicating with them. It's actually my only talent.

I come from a long line of witches and warlocks. My sister Jess is a whiz at spells. She works at the library and is more of a traditional witch than me. My Grandmother, Grandma Grant, is very powerful, which can be quite dangerous, as I'm convinced she has lost her marbles. It's nothing to do with her advancing years, though. She's always been a little crazy.

My father turned his back on magic, so Grandma Grant was delighted when Jess and I wanted to explore our magical abilities. She was overjoyed when she realized I was a "communicator," apparently communicating with ghosts is a rare ability. Unfortunately, she wasn't so impressed with my other magic skills, which are practically non-existent.

Loretta, through whom I had just walked, is the diner's resident ghost. She had haunted the diner for years as far as I can tell, long before I started working here. A few months ago, I tried to ask her when she'd become a ghost, but she'd looked horrified and informed me it wasn't polite to ask a lady her age. That hadn't been exactly what I meant, but I let it slide.

Loretta looked slightly mollified at my apology, but before she could reply, the diner door opened, and three women entered.

"Speak of the devil," Loretta muttered.

I didn't need to ask to whom she was referring.

It was Yvonne Dean, the self-proclaimed Yoga goddess. She had visited the diner every day since her arrival in town. Although, I had no idea why. She never ate anything.

I took the plates through to the kitchen and then hurried over to get them settled.

Old Bob, who was sitting at his normal table, almost choked on his bacon as Yvonne waltzed past his table. She seemed to have that effect on men. Tall, blonde, glamorous and extremely thin, she demanded their attention.

I was glad Archie was in the kitchen. I didn't want to see him fawning over her again. It was embarrassing.

The three women sat at one of the tables by the window. Yvonne wore a pair of oversized sunglasses, which covered half her face, and she had a yellow, patterned, silk scarf tied around her neck. On her left, sat her sister, Carol. She had a chin-length bob of mousy-brown hair. Every time I'd seen her, I'd thought she looked like she was about to burst into tears. On Yvonne's right, sat her PA. I'd forgotten the woman's name, but I recognized her from their previous visits. She wore her dark hair pulled back in a tight bun, and her expression was sour, almost a scowl.

"What can I get you today, ladies?" I asked, taking my order pad from my apron.

Yvonne took off her dark glasses and peered up at me. "Why don't you remember my order? I've been in here every day for a week, and I've had black coffee on every occasion."

"Of course, I remember," I said, forcing myself to smile and keep my tone pleasant. "I thought you might be tempted by one of our specials. I can recommend the pancakes, and the lemon muffins are fresh out of the oven."

"Oh, lemon muffins are my favorite," Carol said, brightening up and looking decidedly less tearful.

Yvonne's head snapped up. "A moment on the lips, a lifetime on the hips, Carol."

Carol was stunned into silence.

An uncomfortable pause followed her comment, although Yvonne didn't seem to notice.

"We'll just have three black coffees, please," Carol murmured eventually as she stared miserably down at the table.

"I'll have a lemon muffin," the PA said with a tight smile, and I could tell she wanted to have one to show Yvonne she couldn't boss her around.

Carol put a hand to her mouth to smother a gasp, as though she couldn't believe anyone would have the audacity to go against her sister's wishes.

Yvonne raised an eyebrow but said nothing.

I grinned at the PA, thinking good for you. I was tempted to have one myself.

I headed over to the coffee maker and poured three cups. As I prepared to bring the ladies their coffee, I noticed Archie peering out of the kitchen hatch.

His cheeks were flushed, and his eyes were wide as he craned his neck, trying to see the table where the three women were seated.

"Archie, what on earth are you doing?"

"Is that Yvonne?"

I nodded. Archie came over all embarrassed and had giggled like a schoolgirl every time Yvonne had visited the diner, but he'd never hidden in the kitchen before.

I rolled my eyes. "Why don't you come out and say hello?"

Archie shook his head. "I can't. I've got bacon grease splattered all over my shirt."

"I'm sure she won't mind a little bacon grease on her number one fan," I teased.

Archie's cheeks grew redder, but he shook his head again. "I couldn't possibly. What would she think of me?"

Loretta, who was hovering just behind my shoulder, made a sound of disgust and said, "Men! I can tell you one thing, Harper. Men haven't changed much from my day. They always get taken in by a pretty face."

I left Archie fretting in the kitchen. Sarah, our usual cook, was away for a couple of days, visiting her mother in Rhode Island, so Archie had taken over all the kitchen duties.

I selected a particularly large, deliciously fluffy lemon muffin from the display counter and added it to the tray. As I was carrying it over to the table, Chief Wickham and Deputy Joe McGrady stepped inside the diner.

I shot them a quick smile and told them to take a seat while I served the ladies their coffee.

"Is there anything else I can get you?" I asked.

Yvonne smiled slowly as she looked over my head. I knew she was looking at Deputy McGrady, and who could blame her.

He was nice to look at. I couldn't deny it. He was tall, handsome and a little too cocky for his own good.

"Perhaps you could introduce us to these two handsome gentlemen," Yvonne said in a low, seductive voice.

I couldn't help noticing her change in tone from earlier when she had snapped at me for not remembering her order.

I only just managed to stop myself rolling my eyes. I smiled through gritted teeth and turned to introduce Chief Wickham and Joe McGrady.

"This is Yvonne Dean, Abbott Cove's very own Yoga Goddess," I said, thinking how silly it was to claim to be a goddess.

Whatever faults Yvonne had, a lack of self-confidence wasn't one of them.

Both men seem to be so enamored with Yvonne's cool blonde, good looks they didn't comment on the fact I'd introduced her as a yoga goddess.

I started to introduce the other two women and realized in horror, I still couldn't remember the name of Yvonne's assistant. I was usually good with names.

"This is Carol, Yvonne's sister, and—"

Before I could finish, Yvonne interrupted, "Thank you. That's all for now. We'll call you when we need you."

"I..." My voice trailed away. Was she really dismissing me? I hadn't even taken Chief Wickham and Joe's orders yet. I was starting to understand how Carol felt.

"I'm Louise," Yvonne's assistant said, but no one appeared to notice.

Her comment barely registered with me because I was watching in horror as Yvonne stood up and began to flirt with both the chief and Joe.

Worse still, both men seem to relish her attention.

"You're fighting a losing battle there, Harper," Loretta whispered in my ear.

I shrugged. It really wasn't any business of mine.

Finally, the chief managed to turn his attention away from Yvonne. "Harper, just the person I needed to see."

I smiled. They may have ignored me at first, but at least, the chief was talking to me now. It was nice to know I wasn't invisible.

I shot a triumphant smile at Yvonne, but she was too busy giggling at something Joe had said to notice.

I soon wished the chief had continued to ignore me, though.

"I need to have a word with you about your grandmother," the chief said.

I closed my eyes and groaned. "What has she done now?"

"She's been lying in front of the mayor's car again."

That wasn't good. My grandmother's favorite means of protesting anything she didn't like or approve of was to lie down in the road, disrupting traffic. Luckily, Abbott Cove was only a small town, and traffic was light. I had no idea what the bee in her bonnet was this time.

"I suppose she has a good reason for protesting," I began. "Is she out there now?"

I reached around my back, ready to untie my apron and try to persuade Grandma Grant to see reason.

The Chief shook his head. "No, I've no doubt she would have stayed there all day, but the Mayor's chauffeur managed to drive around her, and I guess she realized lying in the road after that was pretty pointless. But you really need to stop her doing things like this, Harper. Not only because it disrupts the town's traffic, but because it's dangerous. She could get hurt."

I nodded. "I know. I'll have a word with her," I said, even though I knew it wouldn't do any good. Grandma Grant was a law unto herself, and she never listened to my sister or me.

"Wait... Since when did the Mayor have a chauffeur?"

The chief shrugged. "He hired Old Bob's nephew, Graham, a month ago."

I opened my mouth to respond but then arched an eyebrow as I saw Joe McGrady slip into the same booth as Yvonne, Carol and Yvonne's assistant.

"Do join us, Chief Wickham. It's a bit of a squeeze, but I'm sure you won't mind getting cozy," Yvonne said with a saccharine sweet smile.

I wanted to throw up. Instead, I smiled brightly and asked the chief and Joe what I could get them.

"Well," the chief said, rubbing his belly. "I have already eaten breakfast, but that muffin looks delicious," he said eyeing the lemon muffin I'd brought over for Yvonne's assistant.

"They haven't long been out of the oven. They are still warm," I said.

The chief smiled broadly. "Go on, you've twisted my arm. I'll have a lemon muffin and one of those fancy coffees you make with the frothy milk."

"Coming right up," I said and then turned to Joe. "Deputy McGrady?"

Joe looked at me, and a puzzled smile tugged at his lips. He was probably wondering why I was being so formal and not just calling him Joe.

I intended to show Yvonne by example that our law enforcement officers in Abbott Cove should be treated with respect, but it wasn't working out too well.

I stood there awkwardly as Yvonne fondled Joe's bicep.

"Oh, I can see you take exercise very seriously. You should try my yoga class. We could do with some more men to balance things out."

I was gratified to see Joe shift in his seat, so Yvonne's hands fell from his arm. "Yoga is not really my thing."

"You never know until you give it a try," Yvonne said in a seductive purr.

I cleared my throat trying to get his attention again.

When that didn't work, I lost my patience.

"What can I get you?" I snapped, feeling irritable.

Joe looked up, "Uh, sorry, Harper. I'll have the same as the chief. One of those lemon muffins, but I'll take my coffee black."

"Coming right up," I said, turned around, and for the second time that day, I walked straight through Loretta.

I SPENT the next half an hour, wiping down tables that were already clean, and topping up sugar bowls that were already full, all the while, keeping my eyes firmly on Joe, Yvonne and the chief, who all seemed to be getting along like a house on fire. The same couldn't be said for Louise and Carol. Both women sat quietly, seemingly content to let Yvonne be the center of attention. I imagine Yvonne wouldn't have stood for anything less.

Poor Carol had watched Louise, Chief Wickham and Joe polish off their lemon muffins. I was tempted to bring another one to the table and tell Carol it was my treat, but it really wasn't any of

11

my business. If she wanted to be bossed around by her sister, there wasn't much I could do about it. But I hated to see anyone pushed around like that, and Carol looked very miserable.

After I'd finished cleaning table seven, I walked back over to the booth by the window and decided to give Carol another chance to order a muffin.

"Can I get you guys anything else? Are you sure you won't change your mind about that muffin, Carol?"

Carol hesitated, but then she shook her head and looked down miserably at her lap.

The Chief had eaten his muffin in three bites. "You should have one. They are absolutely delicious," he said and then turned his gaze on Yvonne. "Why don't you have one, too? You look like you could do with a treat."

The saccharine smile left Yvonne's face, and she pursed her lips. "I can assure you I am quite sweet enough. Anyway," she said as she turned her head and pointedly gazed at my hips. "Some of us watch our figures."

I felt my cheeks heat up. That was a low blow. I had put on a few pounds over winter. What can I say? I work at a diner where the food is delicious, and Sarah makes the most amazing carrot cake.

But I wasn't Carol, and I wasn't going to let Yvonne make me feel guilty.

I completely ignored Yvonne and turned again to Carol. "Are you sure, Carol? I could put one in a bag for you to take out."

Carol looked up. Her eyes flickered to her sister and then back to me before she gave a tentative smile. "Yes, I'd like that. I'll have one to take out."

I smiled to myself as I walked back to the counter to bag up a muffin for Carol.

It was only a small step, but I was glad she'd stood up for herself.

Shortly afterward, Old Bob left his corner table followed by the chief and Joe McGrady.

The three women remained in the booth, having a deep discussion. I only caught every other sentence or so, but it sounded like they were talking about setting up the new yoga business.

I imagined Yvonne must be doing very well for herself to employ a personal assistant and her sister to help. It surprised me that she was setting up a base in a town as small as Abbott Cove. We weren't exactly a bustling metropolis, and I wasn't quite sure how many customers she would have.

But I suppose Yoga paid well. She had a very expensive-looking watch on her wrist, not that I knew much about that sort of thing, and her clothes looked expensive. I was pretty sure she had a top of the range Coach purse on the floor beside her feet.

It had been quiet so far this morning, and it didn't appear to be getting any busier as we approached lunchtime. Sometimes the diner could be like that. Other days, we'd have busloads of tourists descend upon us, and we'd be packed out. We never knew what days we were going to be busy, but as Archie said, at least it kept us on our toes.

Archie still hadn't dared to come out of the kitchen, which I found amusing and irritating at the same time.

I began to fold some napkins — one of those jobs I tended to do when it was quiet — when all of a sudden I heard Yvonne raise her voice.

"Oh, for goodness sake. Do I have to think of everything? Can you never think for yourself? I suppose this is another mess you expect me to get us out of."

I looked up but quickly looked down again as Yvonne caught me watching and scowled.

I didn't mean to eavesdrop, but if she spoke so loudly in a public place, I would hardly classify that as eavesdropping.

Yvonne huffed out an impatient breath and shrugged on her jacket. "Well, why are you just sitting there? Go and pay the bill," Yvonne snapped at her sister.

Carol hastily got to her feet and rushed over to me.

"Can I get the check?" she mumbled miserably, rummaging through her purse.

"Of course, I would have brought it over to you," I said as I started to ring their order up on the till.

"I thought I'd better come over to the counter. Yvonne is in rather a hurry."

After Carol had paid the check, the three women left the diner. I stared after them, and a strange sense of unease made me shiver.

Loretta drifted in front of me, and as the door closed behind them, she said, "That woman is going to cause trouble for Abbott Cove, mark my words."

I exhaled a long breath. I had a horrible feeling Loretta was right.

CHAPTER 2

THE REST of the day at the diner passed just as slowly. We only had a slow trickle of customers all day.

After Yvonne left, Archie eventually ventured out from the kitchen and good-naturedly put up with my teasing over his obvious crush on Yvonne.

He let me go early. I wasn't sure whether that was because he was being kind as we were so quiet, or whether he just wanted me to stop teasing him about his crush.

The sun was sparkling down on Abbott Cove as I left the diner, and I walked away from the harbor, up the hill, along Main Street.

Even the shops along here were quiet today. Abbott Cove was quite a sleepy little town when we didn't have hordes of tourists. Visitors loved the quaint white houses, stores with striped awnings and gift shops with trellis tables set up outside, piled high with fridge magnets and flip flops.

There weren't many shops on Main Street, but those that were there mainly catered to tourists. There were numerous gift shops and a lovely gallery that displayed paintings of the sea and the coastline around Abbott Cove.

As I walked further up the hill, I had the strange sensation I was being watched. I turned around, almost expecting to see someone I knew to be approaching me for a chat, but the sidewalk behind me was empty.

I frowned but didn't let it bother me and continued my walk home.

I share a small cottage with my sister, Jess, which is only a few minutes' walk from my grandmother's house.

Grandma Grant still lived in the Grant family home, a huge, old house on the outskirts of town. It was surrounded by thick woodland and could only be accessed by private road or a narrow trail through the woods.

Despite protests from Jess and me, Grandma Grant insisted she did not want to move nearer to town. For one thing, she wouldn't know what to do with her collections.

Grandma Grant was a collector, and yes, that was as bad as it sounded. The trouble was, she never just collected one thing. It changed from year to year. One year it was thimbles, which wasn't so bad because they were only small, but the following year she decided to collect umbrella stands. We could only hope she didn't move on to collecting anything larger.

She was very independent, and my sister and I thought she was better off staying in a home that made her happy. She ran her nursery business from there and had a huge greenhouse only a few feet from the house itself, which was where she grew all the herbs for her potions.

I suspected that was why she liked the deep woodland surrounding the house. She liked to keep the rumor mill active and loved it when the townsfolk spread whispers that the old Grant house was haunted.

Despite our very best efforts to act as normally as we could around the residents of Abbott Cove, rumors persisted that Grandma Grant was a witch.

Of course, those rumors happened to be true, but we tried to play it down as best we could.

I turned right at the top of Main Street and again had the distinct impression there was someone behind me, watching me.

This time, I turned around faster, but again, there was nothing there.

I smiled and shook my head, feeling bemused. I was losing it.

Since I had wrapped up work for the day earlier than usual, I decided to pop in and see Grandma Grant on my way home. I needed to speak to her about the lying in the road habit she'd picked up, and although I wasn't looking forward to it, I knew I couldn't put it off for long. If I didn't speak to her about it, Chief Wickham would.

As I marched up the trail towards Grandma Grant's house, I felt a prickling sensation along the back of my neck, but every time I turned around, there was absolutely no one there. I was completely alone.

I made my way through the shady, green trail that led to the front of the house, feeling on edge.

When the large, imposing house came into view, I'd never been so pleased to see it. I tried to shake off the creepy feeling I was being watched and stepped inside Grandma Grant's kitchen without knocking. I did that on purpose. I thought I might catch her off-guard.

My grandmother was in the kitchen next to the stove, chopping some green herbs. "Harper, what are you doing here?" she demanded, lifting her knife from the chopping board.

Charming. It was nice to feel so welcome. "I was on my way home. I thought I'd just pop in and say hello and make sure you were all right."

"Of course I'm all right," Grandma Grant said, looking up at me warily.

Grandma Grant was a short woman, but she was stout and strong. She had clear blue eyes that sparkled, and her hair was now gray. I had heard that back in the day her hair was the color of straw, and she was quite popular with the men of Abbott Cove when she was younger.

"I don't buy it, Harper. You haven't come here for a social call. We made plans for dinner tomorrow, but for some reason you've decided to visit me today as well. And you look shifty. In my book, that means you want something. So do you want to tell me why you are really here?"

"I do not look shifty!"

My mouth dropped open, and I was about to tell her she had a suspicious mind, but I decided not to bother pretending. There really wasn't any point when she could see right through me.

"Is there anything you want to tell me?" I asked as Athena,

Grandma Grant's cat, appeared out of nowhere and wound her way around my ankles.

Grandma Grant narrowed her eyes. "Why? What have you heard?"

That was a bad sign. If there was only one scheme she was working on, she would have immediately launched into defensive mode. The fact she wasn't sure what I was referring to made my heart sink. There was obviously something else I hadn't heard about yet.

I bent down to stroke Athena, but the cat slipped out of my grasp and gave me a haughty look. Athena ruled the roost, and she knew it. Rather than being our cat, I think she saw herself as a sort of supreme being, and we were all her unworthy subjects.

"I saw Chief Wickham today, and he told me you've been lying in the road again."

Grandma Grant looked indignant. "I wasn't just lying in the road, Harper," she said huffily. "I was protesting. It's different."

"Of course," I said, not bothering to hide my skepticism.

"It's an important cause, Harper. One you should pay more attention to."

I sighed and pulled out one of the chairs by the kitchen table and sat down. "Last time you were lying in the road, you were protesting that Betty had raised the price of the senior special in the Lobster Shack. You thought lying in the road was the answer then, too."

Grandma Grant smiled triumphantly. "It was. It worked just fine. I got a discount. It's an effective means of protest."

I supposed I couldn't really argue with that. It had been effective. "What are you protesting about this time?"

"The mayor is supporting the construction of that new resort. When they started the project, the plans detailed a small hotel on the other side of the cove, but they keep adding to the plans, and it's going to change the fabric of Abbott Cove completely. That crafty mayor thinks he can sneak all the changes past us, and none of us will realize until it's too late."

I frowned. That actually did sound like a legitimate reason to protest. I hadn't expected that. Before I could ask her any more questions, though, Grandma Grant changed the subject.

"Anyway, I've got a surprise for you," she said.

"A surprise?"

"Yes, but it won't be here until tomorrow. I'll give it to you before dinner."

Athena wound her way around my legs again, and I dared to reach down to try and stroke her soft fur. This time, she permitted me to scratch her behind the ears before moving away again and making her way to her favorite spot by the fire.

Even in midsummer, Grandma Grant always had a small fire going in the kitchen, usually because she had some kind of potion bubbling away.

She told everyone it was her herbal teas, and I had to admit she was very good at making herbal teas, but most of the time it was her potions. I envied her ability to make healing potions. But I didn't envy her the work that went into it. It seemed to me as if she was constantly chopping something up, growing a new plant or adjusting a recipe.

I was relaxing back in my chair, watching Athena stretch out by the fire when Grandma Grant said, "Don't get too comfortable,"

I frowned. "What do you mean?"

"Well, you can't stay here all night. I've got things to do."

I was immediately suspicious. When Grandma Grant wanted to get rid of me, I immediately assumed she was up to mischief. It was a fair assumption. She usually was.

I narrowed my eyes as I tried to read her expression. "Okay, spill the details. What have you got up your sleeve? You may as well tell me now because I'll find out eventually."

Only a few months ago, we'd discovered that Grandma Grant was making a special potion to make her plants grow faster. The trouble was, they grew much too fast and had ended up smashing through the greenhouse roof.

Most of Grandma Grant's schemes ended in disaster.

"It's nothing like that. I'm off on a date tonight, dinner with Roland Dexter. He is picking me up in half an hour."

"Oh." I couldn't believe it. Grandma Grant had a better social life than me.

* * *

AFTER BEING UNCEREMONIOUSLY HURRIED out of Grandma Grant's house, I cut across the trail towards the cottage Jess and I shared.

The evening light was fading, and the birds were chirping in the trees as they prepared to roost.

As we were on top of the hill, in theory, I should have been able to glimpse the sea from where I stood, but the thickness of the forest and trees surrounding the Grant house and the trail, made it feel like we were cut off from the town and the coastline completely. The gentle evening light filtered through the green leaves and gave the trail an otherworldly appearance.

I'd only been walking for a minute or so when I had that strange sensation I was being watched again.

I turned slowly, but again, there was nothing there.

I had no idea what was wrong with me today. Unlike most witches, I wasn't very sensitive to things around me, apart from the obvious ability to see ghosts. I didn't have a sixth sense or anything like that, which made it even stranger that I was convinced somebody or something was watching me. Occasionally, I felt a tingling sensation or a sense of foreboding, but I wasn't particularly attuned to that sort of thing.

I probably wouldn't have given it any more thought if nothing else had happened on my journey home, but when I was only a few yards away from the front door of the cottage, I heard bushes rustling beside me and almost jumped a foot in the air.

I whirled around to see the shrubbery outside the house moving. Not much, but there was a distinct swaying of branches.

I gulped. With my heart in my mouth, I edged forward.

Horror movies always ended badly for the person stupid enough to investigate alone. Perhaps I should get inside and lock the door?

But I had to be overreacting. This was Abbott Cove. It was probably a small animal, maybe a raccoon. There had to be a logical explanation.

I reached the shrubbery and peered down, trying to spread the branches to get a better look.

Suddenly there was a rustle of leaves, and I saw two bright green eyes staring up at me.

I squealed with shock and staggered back.

Then I saw what had caused my panic.

A very small cat. All black, apart from a little white patch on its nose.

I let out the breath I'd been holding and laughed at myself for panicking.

"Hello," I said, kneeling down and trying to get closer to the little cat.

It didn't look like a kitten, but it was tiny, and I wondered when the poor thing had last eaten. I moved a little closer. I couldn't see a collar.

I stood up slowly, not wanting to alarm it, and decided to go back inside the cottage and try to get something for it to eat. I didn't have any cat food, but I was sure I had a tin of tuna fish in one of the cupboards.

But before I could move, the cat turned and scampered off deep into the woods.

I watched it go miserably. The poor little thing.

I considered putting some food out anyway, just in case the cat came back.

Jess would probably tell me off for attracting raccoons to the house, who would then wreck the garbage bins, but there was something about that poor little, scrawny cat that had tugged at my heartstrings.

I went inside the house, found a can of tuna and put it into a small dish.

I put it on the edge of the porch and then went back inside, figuring the cat would be more likely to come and eat if I wasn't standing there watching.

Back inside the house I looked around and sighed. Jess would be out on her date by now, being wined and dined at the luxurious hotel restaurant in the next town over, and even Grandma Grant would be off having fun somewhere by now.

I was quite happy with my own company, though, and since I had the house to myself, I decided to make the most of it.

I headed to the bathroom and prepared myself a bubble bath. I then got out my secret stash of chocolate and made a cup of Grandma Grant's special chamomile tea.

Before I climbed in the bath, I took a quick peek outside to see if the cat had come back, but the tuna fish was untouched.

I left it there, in case the cat came back later, and then undressed, got in the bath and reached for my e-reader.

I relaxed back into the warm water, and the bubbles tickled my skin. I smiled as I turned on the e-reader. This was my idea of a perfect evening. Who needed a man anyway?

What did I care if Joe McGrady was suddenly interested in Yvonne the Yoga Goddess instead of me?

She was welcome to him. I was content with my book, a bubble bath and an extra-large bar of chocolate.

CHAPTER 3

THE FOLLOWING MORNING, Jess walked into my bedroom and tried to shake me awake.

I resisted, snuggling down beneath the covers.

"I've changed my mind. I don't want to go," I grumbled.

"Don't be silly. You'll feel fine just as soon as you get out of bed. It looks like it's going to be a lovely day."

Jess flung open the curtains, and I scrunched up my eyes against the early morning sunlight.

"Why are you so full of beans? I never understand how anyone can be so bouncy at this time of the morning. It's unnatural. What time did you get home last night?"

Jess shrugged. "Just after eleven."

I smothered a yawn. "How was your date?"

Jess gave me a sharp look that made her look very like Grandma

Grant. "It was awful. But don't change the subject. It's time to get up."

I peered at the clock on my nightstand. It was only six thirty, practically the middle of the night. We still had more than an hour before we had to leave for yoga. The class didn't start for ages.

I looked up at Jess, puzzled. "We don't have to be there until eight. I can have another thirty minutes in bed at least."

"No, you can't." Jess shook her head. "We are going to walk to the yoga center."

"Walk? Why would we do that? Are you crazy? I thought the class was in a cabin in the middle of nowhere."

"It's half an hour's walk, along a lovely track. It will be good for us, and get our blood pumping before yoga."

I shook my head in disbelief. "You really are crazy. I agreed to yoga. You didn't mention anything about a hike."

"Don't exaggerate, Harper. It's hardly a hike. More like a gentle stroll."

It didn't look like I was going to get any peace until I got up, and I could hardly fall back to sleep with Jess nattering on at me. So I flung back my bedcovers and swung my legs out of bed.

"Fine. But if I have to go on this walk. You are going to tell me all the gory details about your date last night."

Jess pulled a face, and I grinned. I guessed from her expression she wasn't exaggerating when she said it had been awful, and I was looking forward to hearing all about it.

It didn't take me long to get ready, and soon we were outside, walking in the fresh air toward the cabin that Yvonne had reconditioned into her new yoga studio.

"Why on earth did she choose a cabin in the woods instead of a nice studio in town?" I muttered as we walked along side by side.

"Something about being close to nature," Jess replied.

I huffed and swatted a fly that flew straight at my face. This morning, I felt nature was overrated.

I was grumpy. I liked my sleep, and I hated to be woken up early.

As we walked further along the trail, I did eventually start to relax and appreciate our surroundings. The air was fresh and cool, and birds darted in and out of the hedgerows all around us, filling the morning air with birdsong.

"So, tell me about this disastrous date you had last night," I said.

Jess gave me a sideways glance and then shrugged. "Pretty much everything that could go wrong did go wrong. He's a nice guy. I met him at work. He is the county library manager. He's young and good looking. On paper, he's perfect, but in real life, he bored the socks off me. He likes to take part in historical reenactments. Now, I've got nothing against that. Everyone needs a hobby, but honestly, he didn't talk about anything else all night."

I grinned. It made me feel better about my night in.

"What's his name?"

"Pete Bell."

"I suppose you'll just have to let him down gently. Otherwise, it will be really awkward at work."

Jess pulled a face. "Don't remind me. I didn't really think that through before I agreed to go out with him."

"Well, what are you going to say to him? You can't avoid him forever."

"I'm determined to avoid him for as long as I can. Anyway, I was bored last night, so he probably was as well. He gave me a ride home, and I rushed out of the car and into the house so quickly he must have gotten the hint."

"But did you actually tell him you weren't interested?"

Jess gave me a shocked look. "Of course not. That would be cruel."

"They call it being cruel to be kind. You would be putting him out of his misery," I said confidently.

Jess smirked. "And now suddenly you're the expert on dating. When was the last time you went out on a date exactly?"

"I'm quite happy being single, thank you very much. I have no one to please but myself. I'm pretty sure I had a better evening than you did last night."

"It wouldn't have been hard," Jess said grudgingly.

Finally, we approached a clearing at the end of the trail. At the center, sat an old wood cabin. It appeared quite pleasant from the outside but looked more like a holiday cabin than a yoga retreat. It didn't look particularly spacious either. I thought with Yvonne's reputation and wealth, she would have bought something quite fancy and modern for her yoga studio.

The comfortable, cozy looking cabin didn't match Yvonne's image, at all.

A group of women had gathered outside, so I guessed that Yvonne was planning some dramatic unveiling before we were allowed inside for the first yoga class.

I sighed. Trust Yvonne to be a drama queen.

"I bet she is keeping us waiting so she can make a dramatic entrance," I whispered to Jess. "She'll probably want to smash a bottle of champagne against the door."

"That's just for boats, Harper. No one does that for buildings. They cut ribbons," Jess said.

I smothered a yawn as we walked towards the group of ladies, who were waiting close to the door. The cabin was on a raised platform and three steps led up to the door. As there was no other seating in the vicinity, a number of ladies were sitting on the steps.

I recognized Betty from the Lobster Shack and avoided getting too close to her. She held a grudge and hadn't yet forgiven us for Grandma Grant's protests over her raising the price on her senior special. I think she blamed me for having to give Grandma Grant a discount, which was rather unfair, but I was used to Grandma Grant getting me in trouble.

I looked pointedly at Jess. "See, the class hasn't even started yet. You could have given me a few more minutes in bed."

"Oh, get over it. I'm sure Yvonne will be here soon."

Mrs. Townsend, who was dressed all in Lycra, began to limber up in front of us. I averted my gaze. It certainly wasn't a sight I wanted to see that early in the morning.

We walked about a little, chatting to various people. The nice thing about Abbott Cove being such a small town was the fact we knew everybody. Sometimes it was a little irritating when everybody knew your business, but most of the time, I enjoyed the friendliness and security of a small community.

It wasn't long before people started to wonder what the holdup was. Betty was getting restless and started to pace back and forth in front of the cabin.

"The class was due to start at eight," she moaned. "I'm supposed to be at the Lobster Shack to handle my deliveries. I've got my husband waiting there now, but he has to get off to work before nine o'clock."

Mrs. Townsend straightened up from a hamstring stretch and said, "Do you think they've been delayed?"

Mrs. Dorsett, who ran one of the gift shops on Main Street, wasn't known for her patience. She snapped, "Of course they've been held up. That's why they're ten minutes late. Trust you to state the obvious."

"There's no need to be rude," Mrs. Townsend snapped back. "I didn't know they were exactly ten minutes late. I don't wear a watch. I don't like to be shackled to modern technology like some people."

"Shackled? Don't be ridiculous. It's only a watch."

"Did you just call me ridiculous?" Mrs. Townsend demanded in an extremely high-pitched voice.

I looked at Jess, and we both rolled our eyes. This was going to get out of hand pretty quickly.

So I intervened. "I'm sure nobody meant any harm. Perhaps we should all leave. There's clearly been some kind of hold up."

"Oh, no! We are not leaving, Harper," Jess said. "You are just looking for an excuse to get out of it."

"That's not fair," I protested. "I walked all the way up here. I'm just as disappointed as everybody else."

Jess looked at me skeptically.

"Well, I'm not leaving. I came up here for a yoga class, and I'm going to stay until I get one," Mrs. Townsend said with such fierce determination I actually took a step back, feeling slightly afraid.

"Has anyone tried the door to see if it's open?" Jess suggested.

Betty looked at Jess as if she had fallen out of the stupid tree and hit every branch on the way down. "Yes, dearie. We may be a bunch of old women, but we're not dumb. We tried the door already, and it's locked."

The cabin windows were too high to peer into because the building was raised from the ground.

"Give me a leg up, Jess," I said. "I'll take a look in the window."

Jess shook her head and folded her arms across her chest.

She was still annoyed with me because she thought I was trying to get out of going to the stupid yoga class, which of course, I was, but that was beside the point.

"I'll do it," Mrs. Townsend piped up.

She was only a tiny thing, and the Lycra she wore only served to highlight her scrawny arms and legs. I very much doubted that she could support my weight, but she linked her hands and squatted down beside the window before nodding at me.

"Go ahead."

"Oh, well, I don't really think... I mean... What if I hurt you?"

"I'm stronger than I look. Come on, get on with it."

I did as I was told.

I put one foot in Mrs. Townsend's grip and tested my weight slowly, hoping she didn't strain anything. But she wasn't lying when she said she was stronger than she looked. Suddenly, she gave me a huge boost, and I nearly toppled over. I only managed to save myself by grabbing onto the raised edge of the windowsill.

"See anything?" Mrs. Townsend grunted.

"Give me a minute," I replied and tried to steady myself.

I leaned against the rough wood and peered in through the window. It was quite nicely laid out inside, rustic, yet luxurious. I had to hand it to Yvonne. She had made the space look very nice. She was good at interior design, even if she wasn't very good at timekeeping.

I peered closer, so close my breath steamed up the windowpane. When I saw something on the floor, I gasped.

"Well, Harper, what do you see?" Jess demanded.

"I think we might have a problem."

I quickly wiped away the steam on the window from my breath and looked closer to make sure I wasn't mistaken.

But there was definitely someone there lying on the floor.

We clearly had a problem.

* * *

I WOULD BE the first to admit that my dismount would not be awarded a high score in gymnastics. But it wasn't my fault. My ungainly tumble had quite a lot to do with the fact Mrs. Townsend straightened up and clapped her hands over her mouth, quite forgetting that she was supposed to be supporting me.

I should have waited until I was back on solid ground before telling everyone I could see a person sprawled on the floor of the cabin. Lesson learned.

Without Mrs. Townsend's support, I'd toppled over, falling down, catching my cream sweater on the rough wood of the cabin windowsill and landing on my butt.

I'm sure Jess would have been very amused normally, but considering the gravity of the situation, she managed to refrain from laughing.

"Everyone, stay calm," Mrs. Townsend yelled and began to rush about frantically, doing exactly the opposite.

Quite what she was trying to achieve, I had no idea.

"Do you think we can break down the door?" I asked Jess.

She shook her head, and Betty spoke up, "I shouldn't think so, dearie. It looks pretty solid to me."

Everybody fired a hundred questions at me at once.

"Are you positive it was Yvonne? Was she moving? Is she hurt? Was there any blood?"

I tried to block out all their questions and concentrate. We had no mobile phone signal up here so someone would have to go down into town to call for help.

Jess, in her normal cool-headed way, began to allocate tasks to everyone. She told Betty to take her car immediately and go to town and get help.

But before Betty was out of sight, we heard another car pull up.

The parking area was set a long way back, behind a row of trees, so we didn't see the car, but we could hear it.

Everyone fell silent as we waited to see who the newcomer was. I was hoping it was Chief Wickham, but that was unlikely. The Chief couldn't have gotten here that quickly.

From some distance away, we saw Betty waving to someone, but I couldn't quite see who it was. Then a figure appeared from behind the trees and began to run towards us. It was Carol, Yvonne's sister. I recognized her from her long, blue coat.

She ran all the way to the cabin and arrived breathlessly in front of us, starting to fumble around in her purse.

"I've got the spare key in here somewhere. I know I have."

Everyone stayed silent as Carol opened the door. Her hands were shaking, and she called out, "Yvonne? It's me. Are you okay?"

There was no reply, and Carol hesitated in the doorway. She turned to me and said, "Are you sure it was her?"

We both stepped inside the cabin and saw Yvonne's body at the same time. Carol screamed and then clamped her hands over her mouth.

"Yvonne! Oh, God. Is she dead?"

I moved past her gently, and as I approached Yvonne, I saw what I had feared was true.

Yvonne lay in the center of the room, unnaturally still. If she'd been sleeping, although goodness knows why she would have been sleeping on a hard, wooden floor, she would have been woken by all the commotion.

I stepped around her body and saw her lifeless eyes were wide open and staring at me.

I heard Carol sobbing behind me as I realized there was nothing we could do for Yvonne. She was dead.

I heard footsteps behind me and heard Mrs. Townsend say, "Oh no, she's dead, isn't she?"

I managed to nod, but I didn't trust my voice to speak. I had a lump in my throat.

Yvonne wore the yellow scarf she'd had on yesterday. It was knotted around her neck, and just above it, I could see bruises on her skin. I was no expert, but I was willing to bet Yvonne had been strangled with her own scarf.

I straightened up and turned to face Carol and the rest of the women who were gathered by the door.

"Someone had better call Chief Wickham."

CHAPTER 4

I<small>T SEEMED</small> to take forever for the chief and Deputy McGrady to arrive. Jess and I did our best to comfort Yvonne's sister, Carol, while we waited.

Tears spilled down Carol's pale cheeks, and she couldn't stop trembling. I couldn't imagine how awful this situation must be for her.

I was quite sure I would never forget the sight of Yvonne's body on the floor, her eyes wide open and staring at me.

When Chief Wickham and Joe eventually arrived on the scene, the chief strode up, looking anxious.

We had persuaded Carol to sit on the steps that led up to the door of the cabin as we were genuinely worried she might collapse. Chief Wickham looked down at us, a kind expression on his old face.

"I'm dreadfully sorry to hear about the loss of your sister, ma'am," he said. "I'm going to go inside the cabin now. I'll be out to speak to you shortly."

The Chief wasn't in the cabin long. He stepped out again and exchanged a curt nod with Joe McGrady. Then he turned to face Carol with a grave expression on his face.

"I know this is a very difficult time for you, ma'am, but can you think of anyone who might have wanted to hurt your sister?"

Carol blinked up at him and looked confused. She seemed to be really struggling to process what was happening.

I exchanged a glance with Jess, who wrapped an arm around Carol's shoulder and gave her a gentle squeeze.

"Perhaps you could talk to her later Chief Wickham," I suggested.

The chief nodded slowly. "Of course, Doc Morrison is on the way. He should be able to give Miss Dean something to help with the shock."

Then the chief beckoned Joe and headed up the steps towards the cabin.

As Joe McGrady passed us, he put his hand on my shoulder for the briefest second and said, "I hope you're okay, Harper."

I nodded and managed to swallow past the lump in my throat. I didn't trust myself to reply. I was shaking almost as much as Carol.

The Chief and Deputy headed inside the cabin to deal with the formalities, examining evidence, securing the crime scene and making sure no one else entered until the forensic team got there.

Abbott Cove wasn't a big enough town to have its own forensic team, so the chief would need help to come over from another police department.

Doc Morrison was next to arrive on the scene. He was Abbott Cove's most senior doctor, and he'd managed the only medical practice in the area for a long time.

Jess and I hadn't had much to do with him because we'd only moved permanently to the area a few years ago, before that, we lived in New York with our parents.

He walked up to us like a condemned man. I couldn't blame him. He was just a local doctor, used to treating people for flu and other minor ailments. I'm sure he hadn't often been required to examine the body of a murder victim.

His eyes darted towards us, and then he chewed on his lower lip as he gazed at the entrance to the cabin.

"I take it I need to go in there," Dr. Morrison said nervously.

Jess and I both nodded, and Carol stared straight ahead as though she didn't even see the doctor.

Doc Morrison gave us a grim smile and climbed the steps to the cabin.

Although Yvonne was long past needing a doctor herself, I knew the chief would be hoping Doc Morrison could give them something to go on before the forensic team arrived. Anything he could tell them about the time of death or cause of death could help them apprehend the suspect sooner. The trouble with living in a small town like Abbott Cove was that you had to wait for assistance for a long time, and by then, the murderer could be long gone.

I thought it was quite obvious how she'd been murdered. Those bruises around her neck certainly didn't get there by accident.

Jess chewed her fingernails nervously. She liked to be in control at all times and didn't like it when she couldn't see a solution to the problem.

We'd had a murder in Abbott Cove a few months ago that had shocked everyone to the core and to have another so soon was extremely unnerving.

"Perhaps we could take you back to The Oceanview," Jess suggested to Carol.

The Oceanview was the guesthouse where Carol, her sister and Louise had been staying since they'd arrived in town. They hadn't yet found anything more permanent.

I thought Jess's idea was a pretty good one. Although it wasn't a cold day, Carol was now shivering uncontrollably, and I wondered whether she'd gone into shock.

"Perhaps we should ask Doc Morrison to check Carol out before we go," I said widening my eyes with emphasis at Jess.

Jess nodded. "Good idea."

"Carol, is Louise back at The Oceanview Guesthouse? Perhaps we should call her and let her know what's happened. It would be a good idea for you to have somebody with you, too," I said.

Carol looked up at me, and her forehead wrinkled in confusion. "It's her day off today. I don't know where she is."

That was unfortunate. Neither Jess nor I knew Carol very well, and it was hard to know how to comfort somebody you didn't know. I supposed we could take her back to our house for a little while until she calmed down. I really didn't think it was a good idea for her to be left alone.

I was thinking things through when Carol surprised me by saying, "Although I don't think Louise was going to be her assistant much longer. They had a huge row last night."

My jaw dropped open, and I looked at Jess. This could be important. If they'd fallen out, had Louise been angry enough to kill her boss? I knew Yvonne wasn't easy to work with. Perhaps Louise just snapped.

"What did they row about?" Jess asked.

Carol shook her head. "I don't know. They hadn't been getting on well for a little while, and last night, it just came to a head. I could hear shouting but couldn't make out exactly what they were saying."

Jess shot me a pointed glance, and I knew exactly what she was thinking. But would a woman be strong enough to strangle another woman to death? I didn't know.

I knew it was definitely something we should mention to the chief, though.

Doc Morrison staggered out of the cabin. He looked even paler than when he went in. He sat down on the top step with a sigh.

I reached over to pat him on the forearm. "Are you okay, Dr. Morrison?"

He nodded absentmindedly as though he was still in the room with Yvonne's dead body. "Yes, I'm fine. It was just a bit of a shock."

"Is there anything you can tell us? Did someone strangle her?"

Jess reached over to slap me on the shoulder, warning me that I was being insensitive because Carol was sitting right next to us.

But surely Carol would want to know how her sister died. I glanced at Carol, who was now twisting her hands in her lap and looking down at her knees.

I wasn't sure she was even listening.

"This is Yvonne's sister," I said to Dr. Morrison. "She's understandably very upset. I wondered if perhaps you could give her something for the shock?"

"Of course," Dr. Morrison said. "I think Chief Wickham would like to have a word with her first, and then Carol and I can have a chat. I'm sure I can prescribe something to help."

The next half an hour passed agonizingly slowly.

The chief and Joe hung around in the cabin for a long time, Betty, from the Lobster Shack, approached and called out, telling Chief Wickham off for keeping Carol at the scene of the crime.

"Would you look at the poor girl? If you want to talk to her, you should do it now, and then let me take her back to the guesthouse. She needs a stiff drink and something to help her sleep."

Carol shook her head. "I don't want to sleep. I know I'll just keep seeing poor Yvonne every time I close my eyes."

"There, there, sweetheart. I'm so sorry this has happened. I'll make sure you get home and comfortable. Nobody is going to make you fall asleep if you don't want to."

Chief Wickham tried to ask Carol some questions, but he was fighting a losing battle. She was not in any fit state to be a useful witness, so eventually, he relented.

Abbott Cove was the sort of town that pulled together during a crisis, and that was evident today. Everyone was rallying around to help Carol.

Chief Wickham allowed Betty to take Carol back to the guesthouse, but he ordered the rest of us to stay until Deputy McGrady had taken the names and addresses of everyone present.

I felt sorry for the chief. Trying to solve the last murder in Abbott Cove had been very difficult for him, and I had a feeling this one would be even more stressful than the last.

CHAPTER 5

As the ladies queued up to give Deputy McGrady their names and addresses, I decided to have a bit of a poke around outside the cabin to see if I could find Yvonne's ghost.

I didn't know whether Yvonne's ghost would have stuck around. The other murder victim I had come into contact with recently was Elizabeth Naggington. She had stayed around until her murderer was caught, and she only moved on once it was clear her killer would be brought to justice. I suspected the same thing might happen to Yvonne. She'd probably be stuck in ghost limbo until her killer was found.

Although I'd seen many ghosts in my time, I hadn't had much contact with murder victims, thankfully. So I wasn't exactly an expert. I felt a responsibility towards Yvonne, though, since I was the only person who would be able to communicate with her. My only choice was to wing it and hope for the best.

It would make matters easier if there was a way to detect ghosts, but as far as I could tell, there wasn't. I'd seen all the movies and TV shows where the environment would suddenly drop a few degrees when a ghost was present. That would have been a handy sign. I remember one TV show I'd watched focused on ghost ectoplasm, but I'd never come across that, thank goodness!

All I knew, from first-hand experience of walking directly through Loretta, was that you could sometimes have a brief shiver when you walked through a ghost, but other than that ghosts were actually quite hard to spot.

Jess left me to it. We might argue and bicker, but no one knew me better than my sister, and she realized exactly what I was doing without me needing to tell her.

Unfortunately, I wasn't having much luck on my hunt for Yvonne. The clearing was completely free of ghosts.

I got a few odd looks as I walked around the group of ladies, thinking perhaps Yvonne could have integrated herself between them to hide. But she hadn't. Her ghostly form hadn't been in the cabin when we discovered her body, so I had to assume if she'd stuck around, she was somewhere in the immediate vicinity, probably hiding in the woods. It must be quite a traumatic experience to be murdered and then find yourself a ghost. I could understand the desire to hide.

I had my hands on my hips, and I was staring towards the woods when I heard Joe McGrady's voice directly behind me, "What are you doing, Harper?"

I jumped guiltily and quickly turned around to face him. "Me? Nothing. Why would I be doing anything?"

Internally, I cringed at my overreaction. Just act normally,

Harper, I told myself. Otherwise, he's going to think you've lost your marbles.

I looked over Joe's shoulder and saw that Jess was now talking to Chief Wickham.

"Do you know how she was killed yet?" I asked, trying to shift his attention away from my suspicious behavior.

Joe looked down at me, his handsome face stern. "I don't think I should discuss the details yet, Harper."

I nodded. I supposed that was fair enough.

"Are you sure you're okay? You were looking a little odd just staring off into the distance like that?"

My cheeks flushed, but I tried to act normally, as normally as I could anyway. Normal just wasn't part of my personality. It wasn't in the Grant family DNA.

It was nice of him to ask after me, though, and I did appreciate it.

"I'm fine. I guess we're all a bit in shock. It's such a horrible thing to happen."

Joe nodded gravely and then he went and trampled on my warm, fuzzy feelings towards him by saying, "I came over to warn you not to get involved. You know what happened last time you interfered in a murder investigation, and it could have been a lot worse. Leave the investigating to me. Understand?"

My mouth hung open in surprise. For a moment, I couldn't even gather any words to respond. Of all the rude, unnecessary... If it hadn't been for me, Elizabeth Naggington's killer would have escaped justice.

The whole town had thought I was a hero.

Of course, I was quite lucky that Joe and the chief had been on hand to save me when Elizabeth's killer had tried to finish me off. But I had solved the case, and a little appreciation from Deputy McGrady would have been nice. I couldn't believe he was warning me off, as though I wanted to get involved in a case where there was a crazed killer on the loose.

I bristled. "I have absolutely no intention of getting involved. I don't know what would give you that idea."

Joe unsuccessfully tried to suppress a smile. "Of course not. How could I possibly think you might want to snoop?"

Now he really had gone too far. Accusing me of snooping? I wasn't a little old lady fixated on her neighbor's business.

I stuck my nose in the air and said, "I'm not going to even dignify that with a response."

Joe chuckled then and leaned closer to whisper, "Be careful Harper. Whoever did this is a violent killer and very dangerous."

I felt a shiver run along my spine as I closed my eyes and pictured poor Yvonne lying dead on the floor of the cabin. It would be a long time before I managed to forget that image.

JOE LEFT me when Chief Wickham called him over, and Jess walked over to join me.

"What were you two whispering about?" she asked.

I made a huffing noise and said, "Joe warned me not to get involved. Can you believe it? It's as if he thinks I get involved in these things on purpose."

"Well, I suppose he doesn't know about the seeing ghosts thing. He probably just thinks you're really nosy."

I narrowed my eyes and glared at my sister to let her know I didn't appreciate that comment.

My ghost-spotting ability hadn't been of much use so far today. My attempts to find Yvonne had just made me look odd.

"Have you seen her ghost?" Jess asked.

I shook my head, feeling disappointed. "No, there's no sign of her. I'm guessing, if she is still around, then she'll most likely be hiding out in the woods somewhere. Perhaps all the commotion has scared her off."

Jess nodded. "Yes, I suppose it must have been quite a shock for her. Maybe she'll make her way to town?"

I hoped not. I was relying on her staying close to the place she died. Otherwise, I might never track her down.

"I think I'll try to come back up here before my shift at the diner. Hopefully, the forensic team and officers will be finished with the crime scene by then, and it will be quieter. She might be more likely to show herself if things calm down. Plus, when everyone leaves, I can have a proper look without people thinking I'm a total oddball."

Jess smirked. "How could anybody think you were odd, Harper?" she said and reached up, ruffling my hair.

I pulled back, irritated, and tried to smooth my messed up hair. "Cut it out!"

Jess chuckled. "Sorry, I forgot you want to look your best for Deputy McGrady."

Jess winked at me and then scurried off before I could order her to take those words back.

I had absolutely no idea why she thought I was interested in Joe McGrady. I could never be interested in anyone who called me a snoop.

CHAPTER 6

WHEN CHIEF WICKHAM was satisfied Joe had taken down all the names and addresses of the people at the scene, and we'd answered all his preliminary questions, he allowed us to go home. Instead of going back to our cottage, Jess and I headed for Grandma Grant's house to let her know what had happened.

As usual, she was in the kitchen when we arrived, grinding up some ingredients with a gray granite pestle and mortar.

"You'll never believe what happened this morning," Jess said as we walked in.

She sat down at the kitchen table, looking expectantly at Grandma Grant.

"You mean the fact that Yvonne Dean, the yoga lady, is dead?" Grandma Grant deadpanned.

She didn't even look up from her pestle and mortar.

I slid into the chair opposite Jess, and we exchanged a look. How on earth did she know already? That was some serious witch-craft. Had she used some kind of spell or a crystal ball? I'd never known her to use a crystal ball. In fact, I'd always thought they were a myth.

"Have you been casting spells to see into the future?" I demanded.

Grandma Grant finally looked up. "No, Harper. And if you had studied your spells like a good witch is supposed to, you would know that doesn't work. Looking into the future with spells is very dangerous and hardly ever works."

"Then how did you know?" Jess asked.

"The usual way. The Abbott Cove grapevine. Leticia Markham dropped in for some plants earlier, and she told me."

I rolled my eyes. We should have guessed. Honestly, nothing happened in this town without everybody knowing about it within a split second.

"You probably know more than us," I grumbled. "I asked Deputy McGrady how Yvonne had been killed, and he wouldn't tell me. Although I think it was obvious she had been strangled with her silk scarf. I saw some nasty bruises around her neck."

"It was bound to happen sooner or later," Grandma Grant said as she began to pound the herbs ferociously into a pulp.

A frown puckered Jess's forehead and she asked, "What do you mean?"

"Being that flexible just isn't natural," Grandma Grant said with a completely straight face.

"Yoga didn't kill her!" Jess practically shouted the words. "She was strangled!"

Grandma Grant gave her a cool look. "I didn't say yoga killed her. I said being that flexible wasn't natural."

"Being bendy didn't lead to her death, Grandma," I said as I sensed Jess was starting to lose her temper.

Jess threw her hands in the air, and I took that as a signal that she was giving up. I didn't blame her. Sometimes it was very hard to work out how Grandma Grant's logic process worked.

"Did you find the ghost?" Grandma Grant asked me as Jess got up from the table and filled the coffee pot at the sink.

I sighed. "There was no sign of her. Perhaps she just passed and didn't become a ghost," I suggested.

"Not very likely," Grandma Grant said, shaking her head. "The more violent a person's death is, the more likely it is for their ghost to stick around. I'm sure she'll turn up soon. You should probably keep an eye out for her, Harper."

I nodded. "I intend to."

As Jess prepared the coffee, I asked Grandma Grant about the little cat I'd seen last night.

"I don't suppose you've seen it, have you? It was a tiny little thing, and I think it must have been starving. I left a bowl of tuna fish out for it last night but forgot to have a look this morning to see if it had been eaten." I looked pointedly at Jess. "It slipped my mind because Jess got me up so early."

"Are you ever going to let that drop, Harper?"

I smiled. "Maybe sometime next year."

"Interesting," Grandma Grant said.

Jess and I exchanged a look. We weren't quite sure what

Grandma Grant was referring to. Me holding a grudge for a year? Or the stray cat?

"What's interesting?" Jess asked as she put two mugs of coffee on the table. Grandma Grant always kept coffee in the house because Jess and I loved it, but she never touched the stuff, preferring to stick to her herbal teas. As usual, she had half a mug sitting on the countertop beside her. I don't think I'd ever seen her drink plain water in all the years I could remember.

"The cat. The way it followed you, Harper. It could be a sign."

"A sign? A sign of what?"

Grandma Grant nodded to herself. "Yes, very interesting."

Jess took a sip of her coffee and then put it back down on the table with a clunk. "Grandma, we have absolutely no idea what you're talking about."

"Well, they say a witch doesn't find her cat. Her cat finds her."

"So you think that little stray is my cat? It's found me?"

Grandma Grant nodded. "Possibly. It's a rite of passage, Harper. A real witch always has a cat."

"I've never heard of anything so ridiculous in my life. It was just a stray cat. It doesn't mean anything. It doesn't mean you're more of a witch because a mangy, starving cat followed you home."

"It wasn't mangy," I said, defending the cat, and then I smirked at Jess's insecurity. Usually, it was the other way around. Jess was the witch who could do no wrong. She was perfect at casting spells and making potions, and she read about the history of witchcraft just for fun. That was something I could never understand. Reading one page of those large, leather-bound books she loved, would send me to sleep in an instant.

Jess narrowed her eyes. "I don't know why you're smirking."

I broke out into a proper grin then. "Yes, you do. You're just jealous because the cat followed me home and not you."

Jess rolled her eyes again and picked up her coffee. "That's ridiculous. Honestly, sometimes I think my whole family is crazy."

Before we could talk about the cat anymore there was a knock at Grandma Grant's front door, and as she bustled off to answer it, Jess leaned forward over the kitchen table, ready to give me another piece of her mind.

"It's just a stray cat, Harper. And you shouldn't leave food out. It will attract raccoons," Jess began, ready to launch into a long nagging session, but suddenly she stopped talking mid-sentence and ducked beneath the kitchen counter.

I was so startled that for a moment I didn't move, and then I peered around the corner and said, "What are you doing?"

Jess pressed a finger to her lips and shushed me urgently, and that's when I heard the voice coming from the hallway.

The visitor was talking to Grandma Grant.

"I'm very sorry to drop in unannounced like this. It's just that Jessica hasn't been answering my calls today, and I wanted to make sure she was okay."

I saw the blood drain from Jess's face, and it was all I could do to not explode in laughter.

As Grandma Grant led the visitor into the kitchen, Jess froze.

Luckily for her, from where she was crouching behind the counter, the new arrival couldn't see her.

"This is Pete, Jess's date from last night," Grandma Grant said, introducing him to me. "And this is Harper, Jess's sister."

I walked towards him and held out my hand. "It's nice to meet you. Jess was just talking about you this morning."

"Really?" His face lit up, and I felt mean.

He seemed like a nice guy, good-looking in a fresh-faced way. His hair was carefully styled, and he was clean-shaven.

"So, Jessica is okay then?"

I nodded. "Yes. Unfortunately, we got caught up with something this morning, but I'm sure she'll get back to you as soon as she has the time."

Pete nodded and looked hopeful. "That is good news. I have to admit after she hurried off so quickly last night, I did think perhaps she wasn't interested in seeing me again."

My gaze drifted down to Jess. She really wasn't being very fair. Poor Pete. I was starting to feel sorry for him.

Unfortunately, Grandma Grant didn't share my scruples, and she smiled at him. "Why don't you try chocolates? Jess loves chocolates. You could drop them off here, and I'll make sure she gets them. We're very close."

I shook my head in disbelief.

Jess was now making frantic hand signals beneath the kitchen counter, desperately trying to make us get rid of Pete, but that was easier said than done.

"If you don't mind, I think I might stick around until Jess gets back," he said.

Jess made a strange whimpering sound. Pete looked startled and looked around the kitchen for the source of the noise.

I cleared my throat. "I'm not sure that's a very good idea, Pete. She might not be back for some time, and we don't actually live here. This is our grandmother's house."

Pete smiled cheerfully. "Oh, that's all right. I don't mind waiting. Jess mentioned she was coming to your grandmother's for dinner tonight. So I'm prepared to wait here all day if I have to."

I desperately tried to think of another way to get rid of him. He seemed quite oblivious to my attempt to get shot of him politely.

But I needn't have worried. Grandma Grant always had a way to get what she wanted.

"Well," she said and eyed him critically. "I suppose you could stick around, but I'm about to do a session of my naked yoga, and I'm afraid if you want to stay, you'll need to participate."

I shouldn't have laughed, but I couldn't help sniggering. Poor Pete didn't know where to look. His eyes bulged out on stalks, and then he glanced up at the ceiling, refusing to meet Grandma Grant's gaze.

"Oh, thank you very much for the offer, but... goodness me, is that the time? I really should be going... so sorry to have troubled you. Please, let Jess know I called," he said, and with that, he scurried off towards the front door.

CHAPTER 7

AFTER PETE HAD SCARPERED, and I managed to dry my tears and stop laughing, Jess and I went back to our cottage. I let her know I thought she was being very mean to Pete, and she promised that she would call him and tell him she didn't think things would work out between them.

An hour later, I decided to hike back up the hill. I had a shift at the diner that afternoon, so if I didn't go and look for Yvonne soon, I wouldn't be able to do it until the evening, and I didn't fancy stumbling around in the woods in the dark.

As I trudged up the hill, I thought I must be crazy doing the steep walk twice in one day. The scenery was actually quite pleasant, though, and I started to relax, breathing in the sweet scent of blossom. If I wasn't careful, I might actually start to like exercise. Yeah, maybe not. That wasn't ever going to happen.

Unfortunately, as soon as I got to the clearing I could see that the forensics team were still there. There were two large vans, and scientists were milling around in white suits. Still, that didn't stop me looking for Yvonne in the woods, and that was where I suspected she might be anyway.

Walking uphill on the trail had warmed me up, but the temperature underneath the tree canopies was cooler. The wood made me feel like I was entering another world. Even the sound of the ocean was muffled.

I suppose I could have called out Yvonne's name to try and draw her attention, but I certainly didn't want to attract the attention of anyone else, so I decided to keep quiet and keep my eyes open.

I made sure that I kept the clearing on my right-hand side at all times. It was so easy to get lost in a dense wood.

I hadn't gone very far when I experienced the sensation of being watched again. I paused and then very slowly turned around.

There, peeking out from behind a large bush, was the tiny cat from last night.

I had to admit I was very glad to see it was okay.

I kneeled down, being careful not to make any sudden movements that could startle the cat.

"Did you eat that tuna fish I left you last night?"

The cat tilted his head and looked up at me with its big, green eyes.

Considering it was a stray, it was remarkably well-groomed. It had gleaming black fur apart from a slight smudge of white beside its nose.

Just when I thought I might be able to get a little closer and gain the cat's trust, I heard a loud wail.

The cat heard it too and darted for cover.

I stood up quickly and looked around. I don't know why I hadn't spotted her before, but only a few feet away, hovering beside an overturned log, was Yvonne.

I approached her slowly, almost the same way as I had the cat. The last thing I wanted to do was give Yvonne any excuse to dart off into the shrubbery.

But Yvonne didn't move. In fact, she raised her head and stared hard at me as I walked forward.

I stopped a short distance away and said softly, "Yvonne, I'm so glad I found you."

Yvonne's eyes narrowed, and she pursed her lips, looking me up and down.

Finally, she said, "So you can see me at least. Nobody else can."

This was always the tricky part — telling someone who'd just died they were a ghost. Sometimes, they didn't want to believe it.

"No one else can see you because you're a ghost, Yvonne," I said carefully, not wanting to alarm her.

Yvonne shook her head impatiently. "I know that."

I nodded. That was good. She knew she was a ghost, at least. That was a positive start.

"Oh, I'm glad you realized. I thought it might be hard to break the news."

Yvonne made an impatient gesture and said, "I'm floating a foot off the ground, and I'm partially transparent. I'd say that was a rather large clue, wouldn't you?"

"Well, I suppose when you put it like that… But it must have been a shock. Do you remember what happened?"

Yvonne pulled a face and shook her head. "I've been trying to remember, but I can't. There's nothing there." She raised a hand to tap her forehead, but her hand traveled right through her head, and she grimaced.

I supposed that would take some getting used to.

"So you can't remember who killed you?"

Yvonne's eyes widened dramatically. "Someone killed me?"

I waited for a moment before answering. What did she think had happened? Surely, she had seen the forensic crime scene officers crawling all over the cabin.

I nodded. "Yes, that's why all those people are at the cabin now. They are trying to find out who did it. Do you remember?"

Yvonne shook her head, and I sighed. Of course, she couldn't remember. That would be too easy, wouldn't it?

Since Yvonne didn't look like she was about to bolt, and didn't appear to be scared of me at all, I decided to sit down on the log beside her.

She was quiet for a moment. I didn't bother her with any more questions. I waited for her to process the fact she'd been murdered.

"How was I killed?" she asked eventually.

I grimaced, not really wanting to tell her, but I supposed she had the right to know. "I think you were strangled with your scarf."

Yvonne's face took on an indignant expression. "My scarf? My Hermes scarf?" She looked absolutely scandalized.

I nodded. I wasn't sure why she seemed more upset over the fact someone had dared to touch her expensive fashion accessory than the fact someone had taken her life.

"What I don't understand is, why am I still here? Am I being punished? I can't imagine what I've done to be punished? I was always good and kind to everybody."

I raised an eyebrow. Well, that was certainly a matter for debate, but I wasn't going to argue about it now.

"I'm not an expert, but I think sometimes people stick around as ghosts until things are resolved."

"Until they find my killer, you mean?"

I nodded, and Yvonne took a moment to think things over.

She turned to me and looked at me intently. "How come you can see me when nobody else can?"

That was a good question. One I didn't really have the answer to. At least I didn't have a short answer. "I'm… Different."

Yvonne raised an eyebrow. "You're weird."

I scowled. How come I never got to help polite ghosts? Why did I always get the mean ones?

I folded my arms and stood up. I was very tempted to leave Yvonne exactly where I'd found her.

* * *

I DIDN'T LEAVE Yvonne there, of course. I wasn't cruel. I decided to give her some leeway, since she had only just become a ghost and the transition must have been difficult.

"I have to go to work at the diner this afternoon. You can come with me if you like, or you can stay here. But I'm the only one who's going to be able to see you and hear what you say, so I think it's a good idea if you stick with me."

Yvonne shrugged. "Well, it's not like I've got anything better to do."

It didn't seem as though I was going to get any thanks from Yvonne. I was going to have to lower my expectations.

I started to retrace my route through the woods. "Come on then, it's this way, back to the trail."

Yvonne floated beside me, bombarding me with questions about being a ghost, most of which I couldn't answer.

I did the best I could, though.

We were almost back at the trail when Yvonne floated through a tree. "Oh, my! That felt very peculiar!"

I almost envied Yvonne the ability to zoom through the trees like she did. As I climbed over tree roots and patches of nettles, trying to keep up with Yvonne, I got very out of breath.

Huffing and puffing, we finally emerged on the trail.

Yvonne turned to me, looking at me critically. "Really, Harper, you're not very fit. You really should exercise more."

I managed to bite my tongue, but I was liking Yvonne less and less, and I hadn't liked her very much to start with anyway.

I decided I didn't have time to go home before work, so we headed straight for the diner, and as we walked —well, I walked, and Yvonne hovered— I attempted to explain about Loretta, the diner's resident ghost.

"You'll like Loretta," I said, although I knew that was stretching things. Loretta was definitely a no-nonsense type of ghost, and it was more likely that she and Yvonne would hate each other on sight. I knew it was cruel of me, but I actually hoped Loretta might put Yvonne in her place and make her a little easier to deal with.

"Loretta has been a ghost for years, and she lives at the diner. She should be able to explain things to you, things I don't understand. I'm sure she can help."

"She's been a ghost for years?"

"Yes, that's right. She's an old hand at this whole being a ghost thing. She'll be able to answer all your questions."

Yvonne shook her head. "That's not what I mean. Are you telling me I'm going to be stuck like this? Will I be a ghost for years?"

"I don't think so. I think when you get everything resolved, you'll move on."

"Then why is Loretta still a ghost? Did they never find her killer?"

I shook my head. "It's not any of my business. You can ask her yourself if you like. But you might be taking your life into your own hands. Loretta doesn't like people prying into her business."

Yvonne shook her head as she hovered beside me, muttering about how unfair the situation was.

As we left the trail and started to walk through a quiet residential area, I turned to Yvonne.

"Now, I know you have a lot of questions, and you want to talk to me because I'm the only person who can see you, but I can't talk to you in public because I'll look like a complete nutcase. I don't want anyone to hear or see me interacting with you, do you understand?"

"I'm not stupid," Yvonne snapped.

"Fine. I just thought I'd warn you. When we are in the diner, I won't talk to you, okay?"

Yvonne nodded. "Fine."

"Loretta will keep you busy, and once we get back to my house, tonight, you can ask all the questions you want."

Yvonne took my advice to heart as we walked along Main Street and didn't talk to me at all.

I caught her eye as I pushed open the door to the diner and tried to give her a small reassuring smile, but she didn't look too anxious. Perhaps that was because she hadn't yet met Loretta.

The diner was quiet, thankfully, and as I rushed into the back room to get ready, Loretta floated through the wall.

She looked down her nose at Yvonne. "Oh, I see you've brought me another little pet."

Yvonne immediately bristled. "I'm nobody's pet!"

I held up my hands. "Don't start. I need you two to get along. Loretta, Yvonne is a very new ghost. She only died a few hours ago, so she'll probably have a lot of questions for you. I would really be grateful if you could keep an eye on her for me. I wouldn't trust anyone else. Nobody knows more about being a ghost than you."

Despite herself, Loretta preened at my compliment. "Well, I suppose that is true. I'm sure I could clear my schedule to spare a little time for Yvonne."

"I don't need a babysitter," Yvonne muttered moodily.

I shot her a death glare and then turned back to Loretta, "Thank you very much, Loretta. I really appreciate it."

And then I rushed out of the back room, reaching for my apron and heading off to find Archie in the kitchen.

The diner started to fill up not long after I left the two ghosts to their own devices, and Archie and I were rushed off our feet. I didn't really have much time to dwell on Yvonne's predicament. I was glad I had Loretta to help me look after her. Whatever Yvonne believed, a new ghost did need babysitting as far as I was concerned.

I was serving a customer a large slice of coconut supreme pie, when Loretta rushed through the diner, zoomed up to me and hissed in my ear. "That woman is unbearable!"

And before I could react, she was off again, floating back through the wall. I guessed she was going to sulk in the stockroom. That's what she always did when she was angry.

For goodness sake. Why couldn't they have gotten along for a little while? Was it really so hard to be civil to each other? I didn't have time for tantrums. I had another two orders waiting for me at the kitchen hatch.

I served my other customers as quickly as I could and topped up their drinks before going in search of Yvonne.

She was hovering in the back room where I'd left her.

"What did you do?" I demanded.

"Me? Why do you immediately assume it was me?"

"Because Loretta was prepared to help you and answer your

questions, so you must've done something to upset her." I folded my arms over my chest. "So tell me what you did?"

Yvonne looked sulky. "Nothing. I just mentioned she might want to update her wardrobe a little bit."

I shook my head and looked at Yvonne in disbelief. Out of all the possible things she could have talked to Loretta about...she chose to criticize her outfit. Unbelievable.

Besides, Loretta didn't really have any choice in her outfit. If Yvonne had given Loretta time to explain the realities of existing as a ghost, she would have known that.

"If you're a ghost, you can't update your wardrobe. You always appear how you looked on the day you died."

A look of absolute horror passed over Yvonne's face. "What? But I had a slice of chocolate cake last night. I can still see the bulge in my stomach. Are you telling me I will have this bulge forever? I would never have eaten it if I'd known!"

I had no idea how to answer that. Some people had their priorities seriously twisted.

"Yvonne, I think that is the least of your problems right now. Let's focus. You are a ghost, and we need to find out who killed you, so you can find peace and move on. A slight increase in your waistline is not important."

Yvonne peered down at her belly. "Oh, so you noticed it, too. I knew I shouldn't have had that cake!"

CHAPTER 8

I DID my best to avoid Yvonne after that. I think she picked up on the fact she'd annoyed me because she stayed pretty quiet for the next hour or so.

About an hour before my shift ended, Jess popped in to see me. She stopped by the counter and waved to Archie through the kitchen hatch while she waited for me to finish serving a customer.

As soon as I got a free minute, I walked over to her, leaned close and whispered, "I've found her."

Jess's eyes opened wide, and she leaned in so we could talk quietly without being overheard. "Yvonne? Where was she?"

"In the woods, feeling very sorry for herself. I had hoped she'd spend some time with Loretta, which would help her adjust, but they had a big falling out. Let's just say it wasn't exactly love at first sight."

Jess pulled a face. "I can imagine it was quite a clash of person-
alities."

Although Jess had never actually met Loretta, she knew her well
enough from my stories and descriptions.

"We'll be able to ask her some questions this evening when we
get her back to our place. Hopefully, she can give us something
to go on," I said, although I wasn't feeling as confident as I
sounded.

Jess nodded. "Don't forget we have a family dinner tonight.
We're expected at Grandma Grant's."

I nodded. It had slipped my mind. But what Jess said reminded
me about something Grandma Grant had mentioned yesterday.

"Grandma said she had a surprise for me. She is going to give it
to me tonight before dinner. Do you have any idea what it is?"

Jess grinned, and I immediately realized she knew exactly what
Grandma Grant's surprise was. But of course, she wasn't going
to tell me.

"I'm sorry, Harper. I'm sworn to secrecy. I couldn't possibly
tell you."

That didn't sound good. I didn't mind surprises usually, but
when Grandma Grant was behind them, it made me a little
apprehensive.

I pouted. "Oh, go on, just a little hint. I need to be prepared. I
don't like the idea of Grandma Grant having a surprise for me. It
makes me nervous."

Jess chuckled. "No can do, Harper. I promised Grandma Grant
I'd keep it a secret. Besides, she'd probably put a curse on me or

something if she found out I told you. You're my sister, and I love you, but not enough to risk Grandma Grant's wrath!"

"Scaredy-cat," I said, although I understood Jess's reticence. If I were in her position, I wouldn't be spilling the details about Grandma Grant's surprise either.

"So you had better bring Yvonne to Grandma Grant's house after work," Jess said, changing the subject. "Together, we can brainstorm how to help Yvonne. Does she have any idea who killed her?"

I shook my head. "Unfortunately not. She doesn't remember anything about the actual murder. I'd hoped she could give us some idea of potential suspects, but she says she can't think of anyone who would want to harm her. I find that unlikely, but apparently, Yvonne considers herself a paragon of virtue, who was sweet and kind to everybody."

Jess looked disbelievingly at me. "You can't be serious. She can't possibly think that. You said she rubbed everybody the wrong way."

I shrugged. "Well, not everybody. Most of the men she came into contact with seemed to like her. Archie had a huge crush on her, and he has been ever so upset this afternoon."

"Well, this could be harder than we thought. Perhaps we'd better just leave it to Chief Wickham and Deputy McGrady. Hopefully, they will have some leads to go on."

I smiled. But I wasn't prepared to leave it to the police, and I was sure Jess wasn't either. I may have been niggled by the fact Deputy McGrady called me a snoop — I preferred to refer to it as having heightened curiosity — but the truth was, none of us would rest until we found out who had killed Yvonne.

I was more motivated than the police could ever be because, until Yvonne's murder was solved, she was going to be my constant companion.

As if Jess could read my mind, or maybe because she saw the panic on my face, she said, "Bring dessert tonight. We can't brainstorm properly without something sweet."

I smiled. "Not a problem. Sarah is still away, but I've asked Archie to make us his berry cheesecake."

Jess licked her lips. "Sounds delicious."

* * *

Soon after Jess left, Chief Wickham and Joe McGrady entered the diner. I got them seated with menus and drinks and then went to try and find Yvonne.

She was sulking in the back room. I had hoped she would reach out to Loretta and try to smooth things over, but clearly, Yvonne was just a stubborn as Loretta. She was determined to make things difficult for me.

"Yvonne, you should come into the diner because—"

"Oh, you're talking to me now, are you?" Yvonne sniped sarcastically. "I thought it was to be silence at all times in the diner."

Her face had such a sour look. I wanted to shake some sense into her. Unfortunately, I couldn't because my hands wouldn't be able to grip her, so instead, I made do with giving her a fierce glare.

The fact I was mad at her didn't really have much effect on Yvonne. She didn't care.

"I'm bored. You told me Loretta would help me, and all she did was be mean to me and leave me all on my own."

"Stop complaining. I just popped in here to tell you that Chief Wickham is here. You should get out into the diner and see if you can overhear anything. They might discuss the investigation, and it could trigger a memory and help you remember what happened."

I prepared to leave, but Yvonne's voice stopped me. "What sort of memory?"

I groaned. "I don't know. That's why you have to go and listen. If you learn something about their investigation, it could help. You might hear which suspects they are looking into, or they could say something that helps us identify the culprit."

Yvonne shook her head. "I don't know why you're so fixated on the idea I knew my killer. It was probably just some crazed psychopath. Why would anybody want to kill me if they knew me? Everyone loves me."

She really was delusional. I had only known her for a few days, but I could certainly count a couple of people who may have wanted her out of the way. She had treated people badly, especially her assistant, Louise, and her sister, Carol.

If that was how Yvonne treated family, no doubt there were plenty of other people in the woodwork she had treated badly, too.

"Most homicides are committed by people known to the victim," I said.

"And how exactly are you such an expert on the matter?" Yvonne said, looking at me scornfully.

"I don't have time for this, Yvonne. Get out into the diner now."

Yvonne blinked at me and looked surprised. She clearly wasn't used to being bossed about, but I was at the end of my tether, and I didn't have time to pander to a ghost.

Yvonne hovered behind me as I walked over to take the chief and Joe's orders.

"I guess you've both had a very busy day," I said, smiling at them both.

I was planning to fish for information and was trying to play it cool.

To my irritation, they made me straightaway. They knew me too well.

Joe smirked. "Yes, Harper. It's been busy."

"How are you and your sister doing?" Chief Wickham asked kindly. "It must have been quite a shock for you both this morning."

I nodded, eager to keep them talking. "Yes, it was awful. Have you managed to apprehend anybody yet?"

"Not yet, Harper. But don't you worry. Joe and I are on the case. We'll soon have Abbott Cove back to the normal, sleepy, safe town it should be."

I smiled. "That's reassuring...So, do you have any potential suspects yet?"

"Harper," Joe said, the warning tone in his voice coming through loud and clear. "We've discussed this. You're not going to get involved, are you?"

That was the moment Yvonne chose to distract me.

She leaned over, so close to Joe that her cheek was practically touching his, and said, "He's ever so handsome, isn't he?"

She trailed one ghostly hand over his shoulder and winked at me.

And of course, I gaped like an idiot, forgetting I wasn't supposed to react in public to anything ghosts did.

Joe frowned. "Is everything all right, Harper?"

My cheeks flushed, and I nodded.

Trying not to grit my teeth, I asked, "Absolutely. So what can I get you both?"

When I took down their orders, I turned and stalked away from the table, feeling furious with Yvonne and not particularly happy with Joe McGrady either.

I hadn't wanted much, just a little hint as to how well their investigation was going. Was that really too much to ask?

Yvonne was still hovering beside their table, and I hoped she would have the sense to listen in if the chief and Joe decided to talk about the case.

I walked into the kitchen to give Archie their orders. I usually just shoved the ticket through the hatch for him to pick up, but I was actually quite concerned and wanted to check up on him.

Archie had taken the news of Yvonne's death very hard. He hadn't known her for long, but for some reason, he'd become quite attached.

"How are you doing in here, Archie?" I asked.

He looked at me miserably. "I can't stop thinking about it. I mean, why would someone want to kill such a sweet woman?"

Sweet?

Yvonne was certainly beautiful, or she had been when she was alive, but sweet wasn't a word I would use to describe her.

She'd been rude, sulky and downright mean to her sister and her assistant. Archie had seen that just as well as I had, but for some reason, he just couldn't accept it. To him, she had been perfect. It seemed as though her pretty face blinded him to all of her faults.

I helped Archie prepare some of the ingredients, and he began to cook the orders as I listened to him go on and on about Yvonne.

Two minutes later, I was actually glad of the excuse to get out of the kitchen to check on my customers.

I felt bad. Archie was a good man, and he had always been there for me. He'd given me a job when everybody else in the town avoided me because I seemed a little odd. He'd overlooked the fact I was related to Grandma Grant. I was very grateful to him, but I had my limits, and I couldn't stomach listening to him sing Yvonne's praises any longer.

I spent the next ten minutes pretending to clean an empty booth close to the chief and Joe McGrady's table. I thought I was playing it cool.

Yvonne hovered barely inches away from Joe, looking at him with a dreamy expression on her face.

I had no idea why, but it irritated me considerably. I was so annoyed I forgot to keep up my pretense of cleaning the table and stared daggers at Yvonne.

I didn't even realize Joe was watching me until he said, "You've been wiping away at the same spot on that table for the past five minutes, Harper. You're going to wear a hole in it if you're not careful. Your eavesdropping won't do you any good. We're not going to talk about the investigation in public."

I tossed my cloth back on the table and looked at him indignantly. "I don't know what you mean. I was just distracted."

"Why?"

Good question. I couldn't answer honestly. How could I say I was watching Yvonne's ghost drape herself all over him? I didn't think that reply would go down very well. I'd be bundled in a straitjacket and shipped off to a psychologist if I told him that.

"Well,… I did find a dead body this morning. Surely that's enough reason to be distracted," I blustered.

Joe gave a tight smile. "Of course, it is. I'm sorry. I shouldn't have been so insensitive."

"We're not used to murders in Abbott Cove. It wasn't long ago poor Elizabeth Naggington was killed. Two murders in a short period of time, in a small town, is unnerving."

Yvonne's ghost hovering around Joe's head was also extremely unnerving, but I didn't mention that.

After Joe and the chief had finished their meals and paid up, Yvonne thought it was hysterical to tease me about Joe.

"I swear, you looked so jealous when I got close to the deputy. You're sweet on him, aren't you?" She laughed, flying in circles around me.

"Don't be so ridiculous," I gritted out through my clenched teeth. There were still plenty of people in the diner. I didn't want to make a fool of myself. I knew if I replied it would make me look like a crazy person, but I couldn't let Yvonne's remark go without comment.

"You know, if you made a bit of effort with your appearance, you might be able to snare him. You could be quite pretty if…" She reached across and tried to tuck a lock of hair behind my ear, but her transparent fingers just floated right through the strands of my hair.

I pulled back and spun around, "Stop!"

Did I just say that out loud?

By the look on everyone's faces as they turned to face me, I figured I did.

I coughed, and smiled brightly at everyone, acting as though it were perfectly natural to yell at thin air.

I could not wait to find Yvonne's killer and get her ghost off my hands for good. This was only the first day. How on earth was I going to put up with her for any longer?

CHAPTER 9

AFTER I HAD FINISHED my shift, I went to Grandma Grant's, marching up the hill and along the trail with Yvonne hovering along beside me. I was too annoyed to even speak to her, but I don't think she'd realized. She was talking and chattering away happily. Even if I'd wanted to reply, I wouldn't have been able to get a word in edgewise.

I was starting to realize that Yvonne had very thick skin and wasn't really attuned to the feelings of people around her.

When we approached Grandma Grant's house, Yvonne finally fell silent as she looked around the grounds and the house itself. From the exterior, it did look very impressive. It was an extremely large house and had an air of faded grandeur. Although the exterior was quite well-maintained, most of the house inside wasn't used. Grandma Grant mainly kept to a couple of the rooms—the kitchen, her bedroom, and she occasionally used the old-fashioned parlor.

"Your family must have money," Yvonne said, and she looked impressed at the size of the lot. "I had no idea. Why on earth do you work in a diner if your family has money?"

I scrunched up my face, trying to summon the willpower to ignore her comment about my job, but I couldn't help myself. "I'll have you know, Yvonne, there is absolutely nothing wrong with working in a diner. And although this is the old Grant family house, we're not exactly rich."

I pushed open the front door and walked into the hallway, leading Yvonne through to the kitchen, where Grandma Grant was leaning over the stove, and Jess was sitting at the kitchen table. We always ate our meals in the kitchen. There was a grand old dining room at the back of the house with a twelve seater table, but we never used it.

"It's a little old-fashioned," Yvonne said, looking around and taking in her surroundings.

She was right about that. Grandma Grant had the kitchen remodeled just after she'd gotten married, but it hadn't been updated since. She liked it the way it was, which was just as well because, although she had a thriving business, selling her plants from her small nursery, she wasn't exactly rolling in enough cash to fund the renovations on a house this size.

I ignored Yvonne's comments on the decor and said hello to Grandma Grant and Jess.

"Yvonne is with me," I announced and waved in her general direction.

Grandma Grant and Jess did their best to welcome the guest they couldn't see, wishing Yvonne good evening and asking her to make herself comfortable.

Yvonne beamed widely, clearly happy at being the center of attention.

"Oh, thank you. That's very kind," she said. "I must say dinner smells delicious. I can't wait to tuck in."

I frowned and wondered when the best moment would be to break it to Yvonne that ghosts didn't eat. It also occurred to me that Yvonne might think Grandma Grant and Jess could hear her. I had a lot of explaining to do tonight.

But before I could dwell on that, I realized Yvonne was right. Dinner did smell good. Really good.

"What's for dinner, Grandma?"

Grandma Grant stood by the stove in front of a heavy cast-iron pot and held a ladle in one hand. "I've made butternut squash stew."

I'm sure she'd cooked that for us on another occasion, and I couldn't remember it smelling so delicious. My suspicions were immediately raised.

I carried the cake box containing the cheesecake up to the counter and set it down. "Archie made us a berry cheesecake for desert."

Grandma Grant lifted the lid of the cake box, and her eyes sparkled. "Oh, that does look good."

"Dinner smells delicious, Grandma," I said.

Grandma Grant beamed happily. "Thank you. It's a new recipe."

I raised an eyebrow. "Really? A new recipe or a new spell?"

Grandma Grant looked indignant, and I knew for sure that the lovely smell coming from the cast-iron pot was down to magic.

"It's hardly a big deal," Grandma Grant said. "Just a little taste spell. You and Jess are always complaining about my cooking. You should be pleased."

"You always told us we weren't allowed to use spells for frivolous things like cooking."

Grandma Grant grabbed her oven gloves and lifted the casserole pot off the stove. "Like I've said many times before, do as I say, not as I do, Harper."

Before I could reply, Yvonne piped up. She'd heard the muttered conversation about spells and put two and two together. "So you're witches! It all makes sense now. That's why you can see me." She turned to Jess. "Can you do magic, too? What sort of spells can you do?"

I realized Yvonne thought everybody could hear her. She didn't understand that I was the only one who could communicate with ghosts.

"Yvonne, Jess can't hear you."

Yvonne frowned. "Oh, so she isn't a witch?"

"We are all witches. I just happen to be the only one who can see spirits or ghosts and hear them as well."

Although sometimes I really wished I didn't have that particular talent.

"And what about your grandmother?"

I shook my head. "No. It's only me who can hear you. But they know you're here, and they want to help as well."

I turned away from Yvonne. Of course, it was very important to discuss our plan of action to find Yvonne's killer, but first, I had something more important I wanted to ask Grandma Grant.

"So, where's my surprise?"

Jess was setting the table and put a bowl in front of me.

"You did say you'd let me have it before dinner," I prompted.

Grandma Grant nodded. "I did. Just a minute."

She ducked down behind the kitchen counter and pulled something out of one of the drawers. It was a huge, oblong parcel wrapped in fiery red paper.

Although I was still a little anxious, this was a surprise from Grandma Grant, after all, I couldn't stop the thrill of excitement that passed through me at the thought of getting a present.

I took it from her eagerly and was surprised to find it was incredibly heavy.

"Thank you," I said beaming.

"You haven't opened it yet," Jess muttered and Grandma Grant shot her a sharp look.

I peeled back the paper, and straightaway, I realized it was a book. Usually, I loved books. I am a self-confessed bookaholic, but I had a sinking feeling as I pushed the paper further down the front of the book. It was huge, bound in dark green leather, and I could tell it wasn't going to be a romance or mystery. Sure enough, when I looked at the title embossed in gold, I read, 'The Second Comprehensive Book of Spells.'

I stared at it for a moment, lost for words.

I didn't want to appear ungrateful, but I wasn't able to muster up much enthusiasm. To me, spells were the most boring things in the world.

I ran a finger over the gold title. "How can you have a second comprehensive book of spells? I mean, the first book couldn't have been very comprehensive if a second book was needed."

Grandma Grant gave a little huffing sound. "Show a little gratitude, Harper. It wasn't cheap, you know. You need to learn your spells. You're going to become a real witch, even if it kills me."

I nodded somberly. "I'm sorry. You're right. It was a very thoughtful surprise."

Yvonne hovered over me, invading my personal space, so she could get a look at the book. "So you're not a proper witch yet?"

I bristled at that comment. "I am a proper witch. I'm just not very good at spells," I clarified.

Grandma Grant began serving up the butternut squash stew. The smell was gorgeous, and my mouth watered in anticipation.

"Harper will only be a proper witch when she can pass the basic spells 101 course," Grandma Grant said, talking into space, obviously thinking she was addressing Yvonne even though she was looking in completely the wrong spot.

"I see," Yvonne said. "So it's something you have to learn. You're not just born with it?"

"Well, we're born with some abilities," I replied. "The rest we're supposed to learn."

"So, is your entire family magical? Did you inherit it from your mother?"

I shook my head. "In our case, we inherited it through the paternal line. Our father, Grandma Grant's son, was a warlock."

I said the words quietly as it was a touchy subject around here.

Grandma Grant stiffened, and she shook her head. "Yes, he was a warlock, but he has turned to the dark side."

Yvonne was aghast. "Oh no! Not black magic?"

I shook my head and said scornfully, "No, don't be silly. Grandma Grant just means he's trying to be pure human. He's turned his back on magic. He wants to be normal."

"Normal is overrated," Grandma Grant scoffed.

Yvonne was quiet for a while then. I supposed she was processing all this information, and it was quite a lot to take in.

Grandma Grant sat down at the table, and we were all about to dig into our steaming bowls of stew when Yvonne cleared her throat.

"I don't like to be rude. But I think your grandmother has forgotten about me. I don't have a bowl."

I put my spoon back down and turned to face her. "Ah, yes, about that. There's probably something I should tell you."

"Yes, what is it?"

"Ghosts don't need food. They don't eat."

"Don't eat?" Yvonne screeched. "You have got to be kidding me! I've spent my entire life watching what I eat, and when you told me that ghosts never change in appearance, I couldn't wait to make a complete pig of myself. I thought I'd be able to eat whatever I wanted without putting on an ounce of weight. Now you tell me, I can't eat anything!"

I grimaced. "Yes, sorry about that."

"What's wrong?" Jess asked, realizing Yvonne was having some issues.

"I've just had to tell Yvonne that ghosts don't eat food, and she is rather upset."

"Just wait until she sees the berry cheesecake," Grandma Grant said. "If she is upset at not eating the stew, then she'll be—"

"Grandma! That's not very nice," Jess said. "Maybe we shouldn't eat the cheesecake in front of her."

"I'm not giving up my cheesecake for anybody," Grandma Grant said and then swallowed an extra-large spoonful of stew. "Yvonne will just have to get used to it."

"Sorry," I whispered to Yvonne. "Loretta tells me it's one of the hardest things about being a ghost. Especially for her because she lives in the diner and is around food all the time."

Yvonne's shoulders slumped, and she looked very miserable.

"If you'd rather I didn't eat in front of you, I won't. I don't want to make things more difficult."

Yvonne waved her hand and looked glum. "Don't worry about me. I've spent my entire life watching other people eat delicious things and going without. Why should I mind now?"

I felt a little guilty as I tucked into the stew, but it really was delicious. I couldn't be too angry with Grandma Grant for using the taste spell, not when this was the outcome.

We finished up the stew and then Grandma Grant went to prepare dessert. She put the cheesecake on her special cake plate and brought it to the table. I got the plates, and Jess got the cutlery while Yvonne hovered beside the table.

"Right," I said. "It's time to get down to business. We need to work out our list of suspects."

"I still think it's probably some random person I didn't know," Yvonne said.

I resisted rolling my eyes and thanked Grandma Grant as she passed me a large slice of cheesecake.

"Let's work on the theory that you did know the killer, Yvonne." I held up my hand to stop her arguing. "Just for a moment. Humor me. Who would benefit from your death? Did you have a will?"

Yvonne shook her head. "I didn't. I wasn't expecting to die so young. It was one of those things I kept putting off. I suppose my nearest living relative will inherit, which will be my sister, Carol."

"So, Yvonne's sister will probably inherit after she dies," I said for Grandma Grant and Jess's benefit.

"Oh, there you are then. The sister did it to get her hands on the money," Grandma Grant said.

Yvonne exploded in a volley of curses. I didn't bother to pass on what she said to Grandma Grant. I didn't have a death wish.

Instead, I said, "Yvonne doesn't think her sister is involved."

"Of course not. She was probably clever about it and covered her tracks," Grandma Grant said. "She probably had it planned for ages."

Yvonne shook her head firmly. "That's rubbish. Carol would never do anything to hurt me. She adored me. If it weren't for me, she would have nothing. I'm telling you, she'll be devastated over my death."

At that moment, Grandma Grant's cat, Athena, strolled into the kitchen. She looked imperiously up at us all at the table and then walked off to settle on her favorite spot on the rug.

"Okay, we will put Yvonne's sister, Carol, at the bottom of the list for now," I said. "Let's try to think of who else could have had a motive. Your sister told Chief Wickham this morning you'd had a big row with your PA the night before you were murdered."

"Oh, Louise," Yvonne said dismissively. "She is useless."

Jess took a big mouthful of cheesecake and then said, "Louise could have held a grudge."

I nodded, agreeing with Jess. "Well, maybe that is her motive. Maybe she was angry over your argument and—"

"Don't be absurd," Yvonne said. "That little mouse wouldn't hurt a fly. She wouldn't have the gumption."

Athena's ears perked up at the mention of the word mouse. She was one smart cat. I often thought she knew exactly what we were saying.

I looked at Jess and Grandma Grant and then pushed my empty plate away. "Yvonne doesn't think Louise could have killed her, either. So it looks like we have two suspects at the moment, and Yvonne doesn't think either of them is capable of murder."

Grandma Grant scraped the last bit of the berry cheesecake from her plate and said, "It doesn't sound as though you have much to go on."

I groaned. Grandma Grant was right. I had absolutely no idea where to start. Hopefully, Chief Wickham and Joe would be having more luck.

CHAPTER 10

AFTER DINNER, I walked home with Jess and Yvonne back to our cottage. I carried the heavy book of spells beneath my arm.

"You can take the couch," I told Yvonne as we reached the front garden.

"Can ghosts sleep?"

I nodded. "Yes, they can. Getting settled on the couch might take some getting used to, but you can always hover."

I had a strange feeling I was being watched again, and I turned around, half expecting to see my little stray cat, but there was nothing there.

Jess fumbled in her pockets for the house keys, and I asked, "Do you get the feeling we are being watched?"

Jess shivered. "No, I don't. And don't say things like that. It gives me the creeps when we are standing here outside in the dark."

I peered out into the dark shrubbery and suddenly saw a pair of green eyes flash in the bushes.

I yelped in surprise, and Yvonne zoomed around to hide behind me.

"What?" Jess demanded, looking around.

"You didn't see that?"

Jess shook her head, and I could tell she was losing her temper. "I didn't see anything, Harper. You've just got an overactive imagination."

"I thought it might be the stray cat."

Jess rolled her eyes as she shoved the key in the lock. "Honestly, Harper. Why are you making such a fuss over that cat? It's just a stray. You'll probably never see it again."

Despite what Jess said, I went to look amongst the bushes beside the house just to make sure the poor cat wasn't there. I hated to think of the little thing being hungry and cold, but there was no sign of it.

After giving up on my search, I went inside the cottage and made hot chocolate for Jess and me.

I needed a lot of sugar tonight. It helped me deal with stress.

I reached for the bag of marshmallows, about to add a second one to my mug, when Yvonne said, "A moment on the lips, a lifetime on the hips."

I turned to glare at her and then added an extra marshmallow just to prove she couldn't boss me around.

It was still a little too early to go to bed, so Jess and I sat in the living room with Yvonne.

I intended to bring up the subject of Yvonne's killer again, because although Yvonne had been dismissive of my attempts to narrow down suspects so far, it was the only way we were going to make any progress.

But instead of talking about who could have killed her, Yvonne wanted to talk about giving me a makeover.

"No, absolutely not. You are not coming near me with lipstick or eyeshadow," I said. "I'm perfectly happy with the way I look, thank you very much."

Jess, of course, thought it was hysterical. "You should give it a go," she said. "What's the worst that could happen? As long as it's nothing permanent, it's fun to experiment. You could do with changing your image. It's so easy to get stuck in a rut."

Yvonne beamed, happy to have Jess on her side. She kept trying to push my hair around, but, of course, it didn't move as her fingers floated right through it. It just made me shiver every time her hand passed through my head.

"I'm fine, Yvonne. Please, let's concentrate on finding your killer."

"But if you had a makeover, Harper, I'm sure Deputy McGrady would notice."

I swallowed hard, and my cheeks flushed scarlet. Although Jess couldn't hear what Yvonne was saying, she did see my reaction.

She leaned forward, smiling gleefully. "What is it? What did Yvonne say?"

"Nothing," I gritted out.

Yvonne cackled happily. "Oh, I see I've touched a nerve there, haven't I? You should let me help you, Harper. I'm sure I could get you two together if you would just listen to my advice."

"No!" I snapped. "I'm not even interested in him."

Jess gave me a knowing smile. "Oh, so you're talking about Deputy McGrady?"

"I have absolutely no idea why everyone thinks I'm interested in him. I'm not. I really couldn't be less interested."

Jess nodded slowly. "Of course not, Harper. We believe you; thousands wouldn't."

Honestly, dealing with these two was a nightmare. Each one was as bad as the other. It was like being back in high school.

"I must say your sister is very intuitive," Yvonne said.

I rolled my eyes.

"Why don't you try it, Harper?" Jess said. "You can get Yvonne's advice on some new outfits."

I was perfectly happy with my jeans and T-shirts, thank you very much.

"You know," Yvonne said. "Your sister has very nice bone structure. She really should cut her hair shorter. Maybe a pixie cut."

I grinned. My sister's hair was long and fell past her shoulders. It was her crowning glory.

"So you think makeovers are a good idea?" I asked Jess.

She chuckled. "Why not? You only live once."

"I will if you will. Yvonne thinks you'd look good with a pixie cut."

The smile slid from Jess's face. "Maybe it's not such a good idea, after all."

I gave her a smug grin. One point for me.

Jess wasn't too eager to stick around with us after she found out Yvonne wanted to hack her hair off. I don't know why she was so nervous, though. It wasn't as if Yvonne could even pick up a pair of scissors at the moment. It took a lot of practice and experience for ghosts to be able to exert force on inanimate objects and pick things up. For the most part, they floated right through them.

"Well, I think I better go to bed," Jess said, standing up and yawning.

I agreed and said goodnight to Yvonne. I did feel a little guilty about leaving her and hoped she would manage to get some sleep. It must be hard to be a ghost in the home of a stranger.

She was certainly a prickly character, but I still felt sorry for her.

I took the huge book of spells to bed with me and propped it up on my knees, turning to page one.

It wasn't exactly as easy to read in bed as my e-reader, but it did have one useful side-effect. I was asleep before I even got to page two.

CHAPTER 11

THE FOLLOWING MORNING, I woke up with a heavy weight on my back. I had no idea what it was until I turned over and realized the spell book was still open and laying across me after I'd fallen asleep reading it last night.

Despite having a massive book of spells sharing my bed, I'd slept quite well.

I left my room, went out into the living area and saw that Yvonne was already up, and Jess was busily making breakfast in the kitchen.

"Did you sleep okay, Yvonne?"

She pulled a face. "No, not really. Do you ever get that odd sensation just as you're drifting off to sleep that you're falling, and suddenly your body jerks awake?"

I had experienced that, though not very often. I nodded.

"Well, that's how I felt, all night."

"Maybe it's something to do with the transition. You'll probably sleep better tonight."

Yvonne nodded glumly. "So, what do we do now? I suppose I've got to traipse all the way to the diner and spend the day there while you work."

I wasn't exactly keen on having Yvonne around all the time either, but I decided not to say so. She'd been through a lot yesterday, and she'd had a bad night's sleep. It wasn't a good combination.

"I don't have to start at the diner until this afternoon, so I thought we could do some investigating this morning."

Yvonne perked up. "Investigating? You mean we are going to look for my killer? Isn't that dangerous?"

Jess walked in from the kitchen, holding two bright red smoothies and handed one to me.

"Strawberry and banana," she said to me and then said, "no better way to start the day."

"Er, hello? That was rude. We were talking," Yvonne snapped.

I thanked Jess for my smoothie and then said, "She can't hear you, Yvonne. She didn't know you were talking."

"Oh, sorry. Was I interrupting? Carry on." Jess settled on the couch and took a sip of her smoothie.

"I don't think it will be dangerous if we are careful," I said. "Besides, you're already a ghost. I don't think anyone can hurt you."

Yvonne shuddered a little at my words, and I felt guilty. It was mean of me to remind her of what had happened.

I tried another tack. "Perhaps we should just go and talk to your sister this morning. Maybe she has some ideas. She might be able to clue us in on potential suspects."

"I very much doubt it," Yvonne said. "But yes, I would like to see her. I know she won't be able to see me, of course. But I'd feel better knowing she was coping okay."

I nodded. "That's settled then. We'll go and speak to Carol this morning, and then you can tag along to the diner with me this afternoon if you want. But you don't have to stay with me. You can come and go as you please."

I didn't want Yvonne to feel trapped, and I believed that a little bit of space would probably do us both good.

Once I'd finished off my smoothie, showered and dressed, Yvonne and I left Jess at home and headed towards the town. As far as I knew, Carol was still staying at The Oceanview Guest-house, which was on the far side of the harbor.

We left the cottage and entered the shaded trail. It was a chilly day, and the sun was hidden by clouds.

Since we were alone, I took the opportunity to ask Yvonne a few more questions.

"Why did you pick Abbot Cove for your new business? You are obviously very successful, so why here? Why such a small town?"

Yvonne hesitated and then replied, "Oh, well I do like the charm of a small town, and I believe everybody should have access to fitness classes. They shouldn't only be available in big cities for rich people."

I couldn't agree more. But Yvonne hadn't struck me as someone with a philanthropic nature. Her clothes, jewelry and everything about her suggested she put a high value on material possessions. There was something that didn't quite sit right with this situation, and for some reason, Yvonne was evasive when I continued to question her about it.

"You could have had an amazing studio in New York or Boston," I said. "Why Abbott Cove?"

"I told you," Yvonne said impatiently.

"No, you didn't. You said you liked small towns, but what was it about Abbott Cove in particular? I mean, there are hundreds of small towns dotted along the coast. Why here?"

Yvonne waved her hand as she hovered slightly in front of me. "Oh, I don't know. I just liked the sound of the place, I suppose. Why are you so interested anyway?"

She was definitely hiding something, but I wasn't going to get anywhere by pushing it.

She had decided not to trust me enough to tell me everything. There had to be some reason why she'd picked Abbott Cove, but she clearly wasn't ready to reveal what her reasons were.

"I'm just curious," I replied. "It could be important in figuring out who killed you."

Yvonne sighed dramatically. "For goodness sake, it has nothing to do with who killed me. Honestly, if I have to rely on your intuition to help solve this case, I'm starting to think I'm in serious trouble."

I bit back a sharp retort as we stepped out of the trail and onto the sidewalk in front of a row of houses. I wouldn't be able to talk to Yvonne much now because somebody could see or overhear me.

But just because I couldn't reply, didn't mean Yvonne stayed quiet. On the contrary, she enjoyed chatting away to me, knowing that I couldn't respond.

Most of her one-way conversation centered on Deputy McGrady and what a good looking young man he was. I knew what she was trying to do, but it wasn't going to work. Yvonne was not going to get under my skin this morning.

* * *

As we approached The Oceanview Guesthouse, I was struck anew by how pretty it was. The whitewashed building had a beautiful view of the harbor. Under each window, there were window boxes filled with cheerful, red trailing geraniums.

I knocked on the white wooden door and waited, catching Yvonne's gaze. It was probably my imagination, but I thought she looked a little nervous.

After a few seconds, Mrs. Dobson opened the door.

Mrs. Dobson ran the guesthouse and did everything herself. She prepared breakfast and dinner for the guests, and she did all the cleaning. She was a very nice lady, but a bit of a gossip, like most of the residents in Abbott Cove.

"Hello, Harper. What can I do for you?" She smiled up at me, her pink cheeks dimpling as she smoothed her gray hair back from her face.

I heard Yvonne mutter behind me, "That silly woman still hasn't dyed her hair. I told her she would look so much better if she got rid of the gray."

It took quite an effort not to react to Yvonne's words. Could she really not see how rudely she was behaving?

"Hello, Mrs. Dobson. I'm sorry to bother you. I was actually hoping to have a word with Carol Dean."

"Oh, that's very kind of you, Harper. I haven't seen much of her, to be honest. She likes her own company, but I check up on her every now and then. I made her my special casserole last night, but she didn't eat much of it, the poor thing."

"Oh, poor Carol," Yvonne said behind me. "She must be absolutely distraught without me."

"It must have been a terrible shock," I said. "I wanted to pass on my condolences in person."

"Oh, did you know her well?" Mrs. Dobson asked.

"I saw both of the sisters in the diner from time to time, but I didn't know either of them well," I said. "They both seemed very nice, and it was such a horrible thing to happen."

Mrs. Dobson nodded. "It was shocking! And you found the body, didn't you?"

I nodded, understanding that Mrs. Dobson was fishing for gossip, but two could play at that game.

"Yes, I was there when we found Yvonne in the cabin. Such a tragedy. I don't suppose you've heard anything about how the investigation is going? I had hoped they would have apprehended a suspect by now."

"I don't think they've arrested anyone yet, but, I have confidence in our lawmen," Mrs. Dobson said. "I'm sure the chief will soon have the culprit behind bars. But I haven't heard any news today. It seems like they're holding their cards very close to their chest."

I smiled to hide my disappointment. If Mrs. Dobson hadn't heard anything, then that meant the chief and Joe McGrady had successfully shut down the Abbott Cove gossip vine, which was extremely annoying. How was I meant to find out anything if I couldn't rely on gossip?

"It is nice of you to come and visit Carol, though," Mrs. Dobson said. "I don't think she knows anybody else in town apart from Louise, and she hasn't been around much."

"Has Louise left town already?"

Mrs. Dobson shook her head. "Oh, no, she's not allowed to leave. The Chief has asked them both to stay in Abbott Cove until further notice."

"Oh, I hadn't realized."

Mrs. Dobson nodded. "Well, I suppose it makes sense in case the chief needs to ask them any more questions. I've been feeling very sorry for Carol. To be honest, Louise seems a bit short with her, and she doesn't have much patience. And the only other person who has visited her was the gentleman who called last night."

That got my attention. A man? I wondered who that was. "Hopefully, he is someone she can lean on in such a difficult time."

Yvonne snorted. "The silly old woman must be mistaken. My sister doesn't know any men in Abbott Cove. And she certainly wouldn't be entertaining anyone so soon after my death. I can't remember the last time she had a boyfriend."

From inside the guesthouse, the telephone rang. "Oh, do come in. I'd better answer the phone."

Mrs. Dobson bustled off, and I gave Yvonne a scathing sideways look.

"I'm not surprised she hasn't had a boyfriend with you around all the time," I said to Yvonne through gritted teeth.

I spoke quietly so Mrs. Dobson wouldn't hear me.

Yvonne smiled and preened. "Well, I suppose I do rather put most other women in the shade."

I turned to face her, my mouth hanging open. "No! I meant the fact you were always undermining her confidence. That's why she didn't have a boyfriend."

"I didn't undermine her confidence. How could you even say such a thing?"

Before I could reply, I heard a woman's voice call out. "Oh, hello, you're the lady from the diner, aren't you?"

It was Carol. She was walking down the staircase at the end of the hallway.

I walked towards her. "Yes, that's right. My name is Harper. I just wanted to pop by and tell you how sorry I was about your sister."

As I got closer, I could see that Carol's cheeks were still very pale, and she had dark circles under her eyes.

"That's very kind of you. I've just come down for a cup of tea. Would you like to join me?"

Mrs. Dobson finished on the telephone and told us she would bring tea out to us on the porch.

When we stepped outside, the sky was cloudy, but it was still pleasant to be outdoors, watching the boats in the harbor.

I chatted to Carol, asking how she had been coping. I wasn't really sure how to broach the subject of Yvonne's killer. Of course, Carol had no idea that Yvonne was hovering between us, and if I'd told her that, I'm sure she would have freaked out and then ordered me to leave her alone for good.

I decided to go for the safest option of asking her about her sister.

"You must miss her terribly," I said as Mrs. Dobson set down the tea tray.

Carol nodded her thanks to Mrs. Dobson, who discretely bustled off, no doubt to somewhere she could eavesdrop on our conversation, doing her bit to maintain Abbott Cove's reputation as a hotbed of gossip.

"I do miss her very much," Carol said. "We did everything together really. People used to say I was her shadow. I'm well aware that sometimes people saw me as a bit of a wallflower compared to Yvonne, but I can say I never once felt jealous. I only ever felt proud of my sister."

I smiled and added a little milk to my tea. "I suppose you'll inherit her business. Will you carry on with your plans for a yoga studio in Abbott Cove?"

Carol sighed and put a hand on her forehead. "I hadn't even thought of that. I still need to contact so many of her friends. I haven't managed to get in touch with them all yet, and of course, arrange the funeral. I wanted to take her body back to New York, but there is so much red tape because of the ongoing investigation."

I nodded. "Yes, trying to make plans must be very difficult in the circumstances."

Carol nodded and took a sip of her tea.

I asked, as casually as I could, "Was the man who called on you earlier a friend who can help with the arrangements?"

Her cup rattled against the saucer as Carol put her tea back on the table. "What man?" she asked sharply.

"Oh, Mrs. Dobson mentioned you had a friend call on you. I thought perhaps he could help you through this difficult time."

Carol's voice had a steely edge as she said, "Mrs. Dobson must have been mistaken. I haven't had any men visiting me here."

Carol no longer looked delicate and wounded. In fact, she looked extremely angry.

"Oh, I'm sorry. Yes, I'm sure you're right."

I tried to rescue the conversation and steer the subject around to who she thought killed Yvonne, but I sensed Carol didn't trust me now. She answered the rest of my questions in monosyllables and apparently couldn't wait to get rid of me.

Whoever that man had been, she certainly didn't want me or anyone else to know about him.

CHAPTER 12

"I SHOULD HAVE KNOWN Carol wouldn't have invited a man around to visit her so soon," Yvonne said. "I mean, the very idea of her conducting a covert love affair after her beloved sister has been murdered is ridiculous."

We were walking along the harbor, away from the guesthouse and making our way towards town. My shift at the diner was due to start soon, but I still had a few minutes to think things through.

I took a quick look around and couldn't see anyone so I decided to chance speaking out loud to Yvonne.

"So you believed her when she said a man hadn't visited her at the guesthouse? I was sure she was lying."

Yvonne looked at me as if I was crazy. "Of course, I believe her. Why would she lie?"

That was a very good question. I didn't know why Carol would lie. But if she wasn't lying that meant Mrs. Dobson was fibbing about a man visiting Carol at the guesthouse, and she had even less reason to lie as far as I could see.

None of this was adding up, but deep down some sort of witchy sense told me Carol was the one who was lying.

As we walked, the sun broke through the clouds, and gulls circled the air above us. I stopped beside the wall edging the harbor, breathing in the tangy scent of the sea.

I stood there for a moment trying to collect my thoughts. I couldn't just go on my instincts. I had to have a genuine reason to believe Carol was lying. I needed evidence. But I couldn't quite put my finger on...

"Are we just going to stand here all day?" Yvonne interrupted impatiently.

I sighed. It didn't seem as though I was going to get a chance to think things through with Yvonne around.

I continued to walk, and as we left the harbor, I saw Sal's ice cream shop. It was the perfect day for an ice cream.

As I paused by the ice cream shop to peruse the menu hung in the window, Yvonne said, "I hope you're not going to indulge, Harper. Think of your waistline!"

I hadn't been planning to buy one. I'd only intended to check out the different flavors, but because Yvonne annoyed me, I decided to buy one just to prove a point.

I stepped inside and asked Sal for a strawberry cornet. I enjoyed every lick as we walked along Main Street towards the diner. Yvonne kept shooting me disappointed looks.

When I'd finished my ice cream, we entered the diner, and I said a quick hello to Archie before heading to the back room to pick up my apron. Loretta soon joined us by floating through the wall.

"Oh no, you've brought her back!" Loretta moaned, sneering at Yvonne. "I'd hoped you would have gotten shot of her by now."

I sighed. I couldn't put up with two ghosts at each other's throats all afternoon. They would have to find some way to get along together.

I turned to Yvonne. "Apologize to Loretta."

Yvonne looked horrified, and she shook her head obstinately.

"You have to, Yvonne. You don't have any choice. She is the only other person you can talk to, and I am not speaking to you when I'm at work. So you can either hover off somewhere and be miserable on your own, or you can make friends with Loretta and have somebody to talk to. It's your choice."

Yvonne stared at me with her mouth hanging open and then she gave an outraged gasp. I guess she wasn't used to being spoken to in such a way.

I didn't mean to be cruel. But the world didn't revolve around Yvonne. We were all trying to help her, but we just needed Yvonne to help herself, too.

After a brief hesitation, Yvonne groaned. "Okay, fine." She spun around to face Loretta. "I'm sorry I made a comment about your outfit. I take it all back. You look quite stunning."

Her words dripped with sarcasm. I would have liked to give Yvonne a good shake. But to Loretta's credit, she decided to overlook Yvonne's cattiness this once.

Before I could have any further discussion with either of the ghosts, Archie burst into the back room.

His face was pale and his eyes were wide as he said, "Harper, you better come quickly."

I followed him out of the back room and asked, "What is it? What has happened?"

"The mayor is here," Archie whispered. "And he's looking for you!"

For me? Why on earth would the mayor be looking for me? I didn't even realize he knew who I was.

But then again... I was part of the Grant family. I smothered a groan. This had to be something to do with Grandma Grant.

The mayor was in the center of the diner, looking extremely hot and bothered.

As I approached, he turned around and glared at me. "Harper Grant!"

I stepped towards him, but I was careful to maintain a little space between us. He looked furious.

This was not good.

"You need to control your grandmother," the mayor said sternly.

If only it were that simple, I thought. There was no chance of me ever having control over Grandma Grant.

"What has she done now?" I asked, dreading his answer.

"What has she done? I'll tell you what she's done. She is, right at this moment, sitting on the hood of my car, eating a senior special from the Lobster Shack, and she is refusing to get off. I have special mayoral duties to perform. How am I supposed to do that with an old-aged pensioner sitting on the hood of my car?"

"Ah, I can see how that would be a problem."

"Oh, you can, can you? I'm ever so glad. Now, get out there and get her off my car!" the Mayor roared.

I hung my apron on the peg—I hadn't even had a chance to put it on yet—and rushed outside to try and talk some sense into Grandma Grant.

But if I was honest, I didn't like my chances. Sense and Grandma Grant didn't often go hand-in-hand.

As I walked further up Main Street, I could clearly see a crowd had gathered around the Mayor's car, and yes, Grandma Grant still sat on the hood.

She'd stopped eating, though. That was a good start, wasn't it?

As I watched, she gingerly got to her feet and began to address the audience gathered around her from the roof of the car. She was shouting and accusing the mayor of participating in dodgy deals.

I'd spoken too soon. This was most definitely not a good start. Bad-mouthing the mayor to an audience while standing on his car was going to annoy him a heck of a lot more than merely eating lobster on it.

Oh no, this wasn't good, at all. Where was Jess? She was much better at this sort of thing than I was.

I started walking slower and slower, not wanting to face the truth and confront Grandma Grant.

I briefly considered running away and hiding. That wasn't a real option, though. Not if I wanted to prevent our family getting slapped with a lawsuit.

I briefly considered running away and hiding, but that didn't last long. I heard the Mayor's booming voice behind me. "Get that crazy woman off of my car!"

Grandma Grant heard him and turned around, shifting her position on the car.

"Oh, here he comes. Ready to do some more deals, are we, Mr. Mayor? How many more backhanders do you intend to accept to get this resort through the planning committee?"

I felt my stomach churn.

Beside me, the Mayor was jumping up and down with rage. "Did you hear what she accused me of. Did you hear that? Why are you just standing there?" He shouted at me. "Do something. Shut her up."

I looked at him as if he was crazy. He'd already tried and failed to get Grandma Grant to shut up, so why did he think I was going to be able to do it?

But I had to try. I rushed up to the car and swatted Grandma Grant's leg to attract her attention.

"Grandma," I hissed. "What are you doing? You're going to get in serious trouble."

Grandma Grant stepped back and looked down at me. "I'm not the one who is going to get in trouble. I'm not the one who's done anything wrong. That's the Mayor's department. He is the dodgy dealer. He was seen by Betty in Cherry Town, conducting one of his secret meetings. He is taking payments to get the resort plan through the committee."

If I thought the Mayor had been angry before, it was nothing compared to now. His face was bright red, and I thought he was in danger of bursting a blood vessel.

He slapped a hand down hard on the bodywork of his car.

"Get. Off. My. Car," he yelled, punctuating each word with a loud slap of his hand on the hood.

"Please, Grandma Grant," I begged, trying to pull her off the car.

The slippery surface of the paintwork played into my hands because Grandma Grant slid off. Thank goodness she didn't hurt herself on the way down.

Murmuring apologies, I dragged Grandma Grant away. I needed to get her out of there before the Mayor had a heart attack.

Grandma Grant wasn't happy. "What did you do that for, Harper? I was just about to get him to admit the truth."

"You were just about to give him a coronary," I replied. "You can't go around doing things like that. You don't have any evidence to start with. What would Chief Wickham say if he'd caught you during that little display?"

"He'd probably say exactly the same things as you are now," Grandma Grant said, sulkily folding her arms over her chest. "Neither of you are very imaginative."

"Well, let's just hope he doesn't find out," I said. "Promise me you won't approach the Mayor again. I have to go back to work, and I can't do that if I'm worried you're going to hijack the Mayor's vehicle again."

"You'll be sorry you didn't pay attention to me," Grandma Grant warned. "The whole town will soon realize I was right all along. But by that time, it will be too late!"

CHAPTER 13

IT HAD JUST TURNED four o'clock. The diner was quiet when Louise walked in. I couldn't believe my luck. It was all I could do to stop myself from rushing over to her and asking questions immediately. I knew that would put her on her guard, and she would just think I was a weirdo, or worse— a gossip.

I managed to control the urge to question her straightaway and took over a menu as she sat down in one of the booths by the window.

"Hi, Louise, isn't it? I was very sorry to hear about what happened to Yvonne."

Louise's dark hair was pulled back in a tight ponytail. It made her features seem even more severe. She looked up at me sharply. I could see the irritation written all over her face.

"It's all everybody wants to talk about," she muttered. "I suppose it's the most exciting thing that has happened for decades in this silly little town."

I was insulted and wanted to defend Abbott Cove, but as I didn't want to get on Louise's bad side, I ignored her comment.

"How are you bearing up?"

Louise shrugged. "As well as can be expected, I suppose. Of course, I'm furious at having to stay in this pokey little town. It's stupid. I mean, do I look like a killer to you?"

At that moment, with her lip pulled back in a snarl and her eyes flashing angrily, I thought she did look like a potential killer. She was the most likely candidate I'd come across so far if appearance were anything to go on. Of course, I didn't say that.

"It must be difficult. I suppose you're used to big city life."

Louise nodded absently as she looked down at the menu.

"I did find it strange that somebody like Yvonne would want to open a yoga retreat in Abbott Cove. I thought it was far more likely she'd set up a base in New York," I said and waited to hear how Louise would respond.

"Well, that was because—"

She seemed to remember herself and shook her head as she changed the subject. "Never mind. I'll have the club sandwich and a side of seasoned fries, please," Louise said, handing me back the menu.

"And to drink?" I asked.

"I'll have lemonade."

I nodded and went to give Archie the order. I longed to ask more questions, but I didn't want to make her suspicious. Yvonne was still in the back room with Loretta. They'd gone from hating each other's guts, to chatting away like old friends. It was rather disconcerting.

I considered going to get Yvonne so she could listen in on my conversation with Louise, but then I thought better of it. Yvonne was a distraction I didn't need when I wanted to concentrate.

I hadn't gotten anything concrete out of Yvonne's sister, so Yvonne's assistant was really my only hope.

I prepared her lemonade and took it over to the table.

The diner was still quiet, so I could linger and talk to Louise on the pretense that I was just being friendly.

"I spoke to Yvonne's sister, Carol, earlier. She seems ever so upset."

Louise gave a noncommittal grunt.

I tried again. "She said you didn't always get on well with Yvonne. I have to say from what I saw of her when she was in the diner, she seemed like a difficult person to please. I know I shouldn't speak ill of the dead, but I wouldn't have enjoyed working for her."

Louise took a sip of her lemonade and then put it back down on the table and studied me carefully. It was as though she was trying to work out my game plan.

"Yvonne and I got on fine," she said, cutting off that line of questioning.

But I wasn't prepared to let it rest. "That surprises me since she tried to push you both around. I couldn't believe it when she tried to shame Carol into not ordering a muffin. I was mentally cheering you on when you defied her."

A small smile twitched at the edges of Louise's mouth. "I've never been good at being bossed about, and Yvonne could certainly be bossy."

At that moment, I saw Yvonne swoop across the diner and come to a stop beside me. "Ah, I see somebody is talking about me," she said.

I did my best to ignore Yvonne and decided to push my luck with Louise.

"Carol told me you had an argument with Yvonne the night before she died."

The smile disappeared from Louise's face, and she frowned. "That's not true. Yvonne and I had a good working relationship."

That was open to interpretation. Yvonne hovered beside me, but she didn't contradict Louise.

"Are you saying Carol was mistaken? You didn't have an argument?"

Louise sighed impatiently. "We had a discussion. I would hardly call it an argument." She pushed her glasses back on her nose and peered at me. "If you must know, she was late paying me, and I wanted to know when I would get what was owed to me."

Well, I hadn't expected that.

Neither had Yvonne by the sound of it. She swooped in front of Louise, putting her face right up to her ex-assistant's, and screamed liar at the top of her voice. It was pretty hard to ignore, but I did my best.

Louise, of course, didn't flinch. She had no idea Yvonne was currently threatening to pour lemonade over her head.

"Oh, that must have been a difficult situation," I said, trying not to flinch as Yvonne swooped across the table and made repeated attempts to pick up the glass of lemonade. Thankfully, she couldn't quite manage it.

Yvonne was going crazy. "She's lying! Don't believe her! We argued because I told her she wasn't pulling her weight. She wasn't working hard enough!"

I studiously kept my gaze averted from Yvonne's ghost cavorting on the table in front of Louise, but it wasn't easy.

"Do you have any idea who might've wanted to kill her?" I asked desperately, running out of options. I was too distracted to try to be subtle.

Louise narrowed her eyes and stared at me. "Why are you so interested anyway? Small towns are far too gossipy for my liking. You're young, you should get out while you still have the chance. Go and see the world. Don't concern yourself in other people's business and become a busybody like the rest of the old women who live in this town."

I opened my mouth to reply, but I heard Archie calling for service,

"Right, I'll just go and get your order."

I hurried over to the hatch to pick up Louise's club sandwich, and then Mrs. Townsend caught my eye at the other table, asking for the check. I smiled brightly at her and told her I'd be over in just a moment.

Louise thanked me for the sandwich and then refused to talk about Yvonne any longer. I guessed I'd burned my bridges there. Louise thought I was a nosy local. She wasn't going to trust me with any suspicions she had.

But I was sure Yvonne was the one telling the truth. She was so passionate and outraged that Louise would lie about their argument. I wondered whether Louise was lying to save face, or whether she had something more serious to hide.

CHAPTER 14

On the way home from the diner, Yvonne and I called in at Grandma Grant's.

It had been quite a disappointing day all round. Although I'd spoken to two people who'd been close to Yvonne and known her well, I was no nearer to narrowing down a potential suspect. I had my suspicions that both Louise and Carol were lying to me, but that didn't necessarily mean either of them were murderers.

Jess was already sitting at the table when Yvonne and I entered Grandma Grant's kitchen.

Grandma Grant was preparing a pot of her special chamomile tea, and insisted on saying good evening to Yvonne, even though she looked in the wrong direction as she said it. I suppose it was the thought that counts.

"How did you get on with that book of spells last night? Did you have a look at it?" Grandma asked as she handed me a cup of chamomile tea.

I wasn't about to tell her I had fallen asleep after reading the first page, so I did the only thing I could do. I lied. I told myself it was because I didn't want to disappoint her, but really it was to save my own skin. Grandma Grant was scary when she got mad.

"Of course, I looked at it last night as soon as we got home. It was riveting. I read at least a hundred pages."

Jess looked over at me and raised an eyebrow. "Really?"

I scowled. Jess knew what I was like when it came to learning spells, but I didn't appreciate her reminding me of that in front of Grandma Grant.

"Did you learn a spell?" Yvonne asked excitedly. "Show me one! Go on, do one now."

"It isn't a magic show, Yvonne. I'm not a performing seal," I snapped. "Magic is a serious business."

Jess smirked, and Grandma Grant said, "It is serious. It requires a lot of studying, Harper."

"I know, and I have been studying. My head is full of all sorts of spells."

"Which ones?" Jess asked me, smiling innocently.

I scowled. Trying to rewind my mind back to last night and picture what was on that first page. For the life of me, I couldn't remember.

Was it something about a truth spell or truth serum? I was sure it was something to do with veracity, or no, hang on a minute… It was verity, not veracity.

"Verity," I said, feeling very pleased with myself. "The Verity Spell, encouraging the truth."

I smiled triumphantly at Jess, and Grandma Grant looked suitably impressed. "Very good, Harper. I thought I was going to have to nag you for months to get you to learn anything."

I wasn't that bad surely. Jess and Grandma Grant loved to exaggerate.

I was feeling pretty sure of myself until Jess said, "Go on then, Harper. Don't stop there. Tell us what's in the potion."

"Oh," I scratched my head and bit down on my lip, trying frantically to remember something about the potion. "The spell and potion combined give the best results," I said tentatively and then felt more confident when Grandma Grant nodded at me.

"That's right."

But Jess wasn't so easily fooled. "And what ingredients are in the potion?"

Oh, no. Jess just wanted to embarrass me, and it was working. I was going to have to admit I couldn't remember anything about the spell apart from the title. But before I came clean, I saw the smirk on Jess's face, and it riled me.

I made a wild stab in the dark. "Well, there's pondweed to start with, obviously."

The corner of Jess's mouth turned up in a smile, but I figured I was on the right track. It seemed to me like pondweed was in every single potion imaginable. I hated the stuff. Mainly because I was always the one told to go and collect it for Grandma Grant's concoctions, and I hated the way it felt squelching through my fingers.

"And what else?" Jess prompted.

"Something about some gypsophila and er...lily pollen..."

Jess collapsed into giggles, and Grandma Grant frowned at me.

"For goodness sake, Harper. That potion is so simple a ten-year-old could do it. You're going to have to make more of an effort."

I scowled and felt sorry for myself. I had more important things on my mind than silly potions. I didn't see why they were important anyway. If I needed one, I could just ask Jess or Grandma Grant.

Besides, I didn't like spells and potions because you were never one hundred percent sure they were going to work. Take that truth spell, it just made the person you cast the spell on want to tell the truth. It didn't necessarily mean they would tell the truth. It depended on how much willpower they had and how strong their personality was.

Jess was still howling with laughter, which I didn't appreciate.

"Don't you think you are going slightly overboard," I said dryly.

Yvonne watched Jess with amazement and shook her head. "I don't think I get the joke," she said.

"Don't worry," I replied. "Neither do I."

"I'm laughing because if you'd made that spell, you would have ended up with the hovering spell on page one seventeen," Jess said. "I'm picturing the shock on your face if your subject had started to lift off the ground."

I looked at Jess in amazement. Firstly, how the hell did she know the book well enough to know which page the different spells were on, and secondly, this was exactly what was wrong with spells. You couldn't even make someone fly. The most powerful spell you could cast would make somebody hover. Big deal.

Since ghosts could do that all the time, I didn't find it very impressive.

Spells and potions were definitely more effort than they were worth in my opinion.

I decided to shift the subject away from spells. It never ended well for me when Grandma Grant and Jess ganged up and tried to bully me into learning them. Instead, I attempted to use them as a sounding board for what I'd learned today, which granted, wasn't a lot.

I filled them in on Louise's reaction to my questions and about Carol's secret male visitor.

"I think they're both hiding something," I said. "But I suppose their secrets and lies could be completely unrelated to Yvonne's murder."

I also sensed Yvonne wasn't telling me everything either, but I couldn't very well say that with her hovering beside me.

We talked things over for a little while, but unfortunately, Jess and Grandma Grant couldn't give me any insight. Although Jess was very interested in the possibility Carol could have a secret lover, much to Yvonne's annoyance.

In an effort to stop Yvonne screeching in my ear and shouting that Carol would most definitely not have been entertaining male visitors so soon after her death, I turned to Grandma Grant.

"I hope you haven't been taking part in any more protests, Grandma."

Grandma Grant topped up our cups of chamomile tea from the teapot and then looked at me and sighed.

"I know you don't understand, Harper. But it's all down to me. No one else in Abbott Cove cares that the mayor is corrupt."

Jess put down her cup of tea and shook her head. "That's a very strong allegation. You can't go around saying things like that without proof."

Grandma Grant shook her head obstinately. "I have all the proof I need. I know the truth."

There was no arguing with Grandma Grant when she got like this.

"Just promise me you'll stay away from the Mayor."

But of course, that would have been too easy. Grandma Grant never gave up without a fight.

"I won't promise anything of the sort," Grandma Grant said huffily. "I hope both of you are coming to the meeting tomorrow. It's at the town hall, and they'll be telling the residents about the new plans for the resort."

It sounded pretty boring to me, but I knew Grandma Grant had ways of making my life unbearable if I refused to go.

Resigned to a boring evening tomorrow night, I nodded and so did Jess.

It was then I noticed Yvonne had suddenly become very quiet. She'd been very animated earlier when Jess had been talking about the possibility of Carol conducting a secret love affair, but I didn't read too much into it. I guessed she just had a lot on her mind.

I was watching Yvonne carefully when I heard Grandma Grant say, "Promise me, Harper."

I frowned. I'd apparently missed part of that conversation. I sometimes tuned out a bit when Jess and Grandma Grant were talking. Sometimes, I felt it was the only way to keep my sanity.

"Sorry? What was that?" I asked.

"I need you to go and check the restaurant in Cherry Town. That's where Betty saw him having his clandestine meetings."

"Why were they clandestine?" Jess asked.

Grandma Grant rolled her eyes and looked at Jess as if she'd come down in the last shower. "Why else would he choose to go to Cherry Town and not use one of the restaurants in Abbott Cove?"

"Well, we're not exactly overrun with a choice of restaurants in Abbott Cove," Jess said. "Maybe he fancied a change from the diner and the Lobster Shack?"

"Humph," Grandma Grant said. That was often her response to a reply she didn't appreciate.

"Why do you need Harper to go?" Jess asked.

"Well, I can't go, can I?" Grandma Grant said, shaking her head.

"Why not?" I asked, feeling put out at the thought of losing my morning to some silly vendetta Grandma Grant had against the Mayor.

"I can't go into that now," Grandma Grant said. "It's not important in the grand scheme of things."

"Grandma, what did you do?" Jess demanded to know, her tone firm.

"Oh, fine. I may have conducted a small protest outside Giuseppe's restaurant in Cherry Town a couple of months ago."

I sighed heavily. "Don't tell me, they put up the price of the senior special."

* * *

THE FOLLOWING MORNING, I was feeling grouchy. I had a life, and I resented having to do Grandma Grant's dirty work for her just because she'd gotten thrown out of Giuseppe's restaurant a few weeks ago.

Now, I had to traipse all the way over to Cherry Town and make a nuisance of myself by asking the staff whether they'd seen the mayor having any meetings, secret or otherwise.

I didn't even know if the restaurant staff would recognize the mayor. So I decided to print a photograph of him, along with photos of some of the executives involved in planning the new resort.

It was easy enough to find a group photograph of the major players for the resort. Surprisingly, though, I couldn't find a photograph of the Mayor on the county website.

I did find one from the Abbott Cove Gazette, which was a weekly paper that mainly listed local interest stories like missing dogs and cats up trees. They had a good, clear photograph of the mayor where he happened to be standing next to Yvonne, Carol and Louise. It was taken on the day Yvonne's new yoga studio had been announced.

I was looking at the photograph on the screen when Yvonne floated up behind me.

"What are you doing? What are you looking at that for?"

"I was trying to find a photograph of the Mayor. I want to take it with me today and show some of the restaurant staff so I can ask them if they've seen him before."

"I don't know why you're bothering," Yvonne said. "I think your grandmother is a little crazy."

I happened to agree, but I had to do it because she was my grandmother. She would sulk for months if I didn't.

I used the mouse to click on the print menu.

"Why are you printing it?" Yvonne demanded.

I looked at her in amazement and wondered whether it was her and not Grandma Grant who was losing her marbles. "I just told you. I need a picture of the mayor to show the restaurant staff."

"But this is a picture of me, too."

"And? Why does that matter?"

I couldn't understand Yvonne's reaction. She turned her back on me huffily.

"It's only a photograph." I wondered what Yvonne thought I was going to do with it and why she was so upset.

"Yvonne, what's the matter? It's only a photograph. I know I promised to help find your killer, but I just have to do this one favor for my grandmother. Trust me, she will not let it rest until I do."

"You shouldn't let yourself get bossed about," Yvonne said.

That was rich, coming from her. Yvonne was queen bossy pants. But I didn't say that. I tried to keep the peace.

"It should only take me an hour or so, and when I get back, we can have another brainstorming session and see if we can pinpoint another lead."

"I wouldn't want to put demands on your time, Harper. Obviously, this is more important to you."

I puffed out a breath in exasperation. "I'm doing my best, Yvonne."

"Really? It doesn't seem like it to me."

"I'm sure I could do a better job if you weren't hiding things from me."

"Hiding things? What on earth are you talking about?"

"Well, you're not exactly a shrinking violet. Usually, you wouldn't mind anyone seeing a photograph of you, but for some reason, you're very concerned that I've printed this off, and I'm going to show it to the staff at a certain Cherry Town restaurant. So do you want to tell me what that's all about?"

Yvonne whirled round to face me, her face a mask of anger. "You're talking nonsense," she spat.

I was clearly hitting a nerve. "Did you ever go to Cherry Town?"

Yvonne shrugged. "Maybe once or twice."

"Who did you go with?"

"That's none of your business," Yvonne snapped.

"It is my business. I'm trying to find your killer," I said, my temper close to breaking point.

"It seems to me that you just like to stick your nose into other people's business."

A moment of silence passed as I glared at her, and then I decided I was done. That was the final straw. I had had enough.

"That's it! You can stay here today. You are a very... ungrateful ghost! I'm going to Cherry Town as a favor for my grandmother. She is a member of my family, and I'm not going to let her down to pander to a spoiled ghost. I'm going to visit the restaurant and ask the server if she recognizes the Mayor whether you like it or not!"

And with that, I whirled around dramatically and stormed out of the cottage with the photograph clutched in my hand.

CHAPTER 15

IT DIDN'T TAKE me long to drive over to Cherry Town. I'd borrowed Jess's car and parked right outside Giuseppe's restaurant. It was a large restaurant that specialized in pasta, and I knew from firsthand experience the spaghetti and meatballs were delicious. The reasonably priced Italian food was very popular with everyone in the area.

It was a large restaurant, far bigger than our diner or the Lobster Shack in Abbott Cove, reflecting Cherry Town's higher population.

It was a pretty little town, but it was set inland, away from the coast, and so didn't get many tourists visiting. The residents were proud of their heritage, and there was a friendly rivalry between Cherry Town and Abbott Cove that went back many years.

I thought the restaurant wouldn't be open until lunchtime, but I was surprised to see they'd started serving coffee and pastries, catering to the morning crowd.

That was lucky. I'd assumed I was going to have to hang around until I saw somebody open up and start preparing for the lunch shift.

I stepped into the spacious dining area of the restaurant.

One of the servers spotted me straightaway and gave me a warm smile. "Take a seat," she said. "I'll be right over."

I sat down at the nearest table, feeling like a bit of a fraud. I wasn't sure the server would be smiling so warmly at me when I had to ask her silly questions about the Mayor of Abbott Cove.

Honestly, the things my grandmother got me into.

From where I sat, I had a view of the vet surgery across the street. It made me think of the little stray cat I had started to think of as my own. If she ever trusted me enough, I would have to bring her to the vets to get checked over.

"What can I get you?" I turned to see the server, who had spoken to me earlier, was now standing beside me.

I'd guess she was in her mid-thirties. She had shoulder-length blonde hair and a shiny face, free of makeup.

"I'll have a flat white and an almond croissant, please."

"Coming right up," she said, but before she could leave, I added, "Do you have a minute spare to answer a couple of questions."

She looked surprised at my request, but she looked around and saw that none of her customers needed attention.

Then she shrugged. "Okay. As long as it doesn't take too long."

She slid into the seat opposite me.

"My name is Harper," I said, purposely not revealing my last name in case this whole thing went south. Plus, I didn't want the server to put two and two together and realize I was related to Grandma Grant.

For all I knew, this could be the lady who'd sent Grandma Grant packing after another one of her ridiculous protests.

"I'm Marie," the server said, and she nodded to encourage me to continue.

"It's a rather delicate matter. I wanted to ask you about somebody who may have been coming in your restaurant to conduct business meetings."

Marie immediately sat back in her chair and folded her arms across her chest. "I can't talk about our customers. What they get up to is confidential. My boss wouldn't like it."

"Giuseppe doesn't need to know," I said with a wink. I wondered whether she would expect a payoff. I wasn't used to this kind of undercover investigating.

"What?" A puzzled frowned appeared on Marie's face.

"Your boss, Giuseppe, he'll never know you spoke to me."

"My boss is called Mark. We use the name Giuseppe just for appearance sake, you know, to appear authentic."

"Oh."

We were getting off track.

I pushed the photograph of the Mayor, Yvonne, Carol and Louise across the table to Marie. I'd folded the photograph so that it only showed the Mayor.

"Whoever your boss is, I promise he won't find out, but I really need your help. Have you seen this man here before?"

Marie looked carefully at the image and then nodded. "Yes," she said slowly and then her gaze left the image, and she looked directly at me. "Are you some sort of private investigator? Has he been cheating on his wife?"

"No... well, I suppose I'm investigating, but it's nothing official, and it isn't anything to do with his wife. I just want to know if he's been meeting anybody here. I won't tell anybody you told me," I added, thinking that she needed a little encouragement to spill the beans.

Marie took a deep breath and then said, "He has been here a few times and always with the same woman. That's why I thought maybe you were looking into him on behalf of his wife."

I nodded eagerly. Grandma Grant would be happy. There were quite a few women involved in planning the new resort in Abbott Cove, and I was feeling pretty confident by this point that I might have something positive to report back to Grandma Grant.

I pulled the other photograph I'd brought with me out of my pocket and pushed it across the table. It showed a large group of the resort chain's senior management.

"Was the woman he met one of these people?" I asked.

Marie leaned forward and peered closer. There were lots of people in the shot, so it was harder to see their individual faces. The picture of the Mayor had been larger.

She looked at the photograph for a long time but then finally sat back and shook her head. "No, it isn't any of them."

I felt the air rush out of my lungs as I sighed in disappointment. I'd been so sure I was onto something. Now I would have to go back to Grandma Grant and tell her that the Mayor had been meeting a woman in Cherry Town, but I had no idea who it was.

"Have you got any other pictures?" Marie asked eagerly. "This investigating thing is quite exciting."

I raised an eyebrow at her sudden enthusiasm and then shook my head. "No, I'm afraid I haven't."

As I lifted the two photographs off the table and went to put them in my pocket, the photograph of the Mayor unfolded, revealing the figures of Yvonne, Louise and Carol.

"Wait a minute," Marie said. "That's her. That's the woman he was meeting."

I looked down at the photograph Marie had pointed at.

Well, color me surprised. She'd pointed straight at Yvonne.

I was so shocked that I didn't speak for a moment.

"Are you sure?" I said eventually.

Marie nodded firmly. "Absolutely. I couldn't forget her. She was one of the rudest customers I've ever had. She told me that I was in dire need of some foundation and powder to fix my complexion. I mean, can you believe it? I've always been proud of my skin."

I blinked a couple of times. Well, that certainly sounded like Yvonne to me.

"You have lovely skin," I said. "Don't pay any attention to her nasty comment."

"Did I help? Do you know who she is?"

I wasn't sure how to answer. If I told Marie her name, chances were she would have heard on the local news about Yvonne's death, and I wasn't ready to tell anybody about the link between Yvonne and the Mayor yet. I hadn't fully processed the information myself.

To be honest, I was shocked. I knew Yvonne had been hiding something from me, but I didn't expect it to be something like this. No wonder she hadn't wanted me to come here and ask questions. She'd obviously been having an affair with the Mayor and wanted to keep it secret. He was a married man as well!

I hoped Yvonne would be at the cottage when I got back because I certainly had some questions for her to answer.

"Oh, she's no one important," I said to Marie. "But you were very helpful, thank you."

One of the other servers waved at Marie, signaling her to hurry up.

Marie got to her feet and said, "I'll just get your coffee and croissant. I won't be a moment."

She left me alone at the table, and I tried to think things through. It was now quite clear to me why Yvonne didn't want me showing her picture around this restaurant. She'd been worried I would find out about her affair with the mayor. I wondered how long it had been going on.

They made an odd couple. Yvonne had been beautiful and elegant, and the Mayor…Well, the Mayor certainly wasn't beautiful, and he was a lot older than Yvonne, too. Still, there was no accounting for taste, I supposed.

Grandma Grant had been correct to claim the Mayor was

coming over to Cherry Town for clandestine meetings, but apparently, those meetings had nothing to do with business…

I wondered whether Chief Wickham and Joe McGrady were aware of the Mayor's link to Yvonne. Was it possible that Mayor Briggs could have had a hand in Yvonne's murder?

Perhaps he didn't want his wife to find out about the affair and decided to silence Yvonne for good. I fiddled nervously with the place mat in front of me. Grandma Grant may have been wrong about the reasons behind the Mayor's meetings, but I was glad she'd made me come here today. It had given me my first real lead since I'd found Yvonne's ghost.

* * *

I WENT BACK to the cottage after returning from Cherry Town, but there was no sign of Yvonne. I didn't have time to wait around, so I figured I'd just go to work and hope she came to the diner later.

I debated whether to go and tell Grandma Grant what I'd discovered, but I wasn't ready to do that yet, and I was cutting it fine for my shift as it was. To be honest, I was quite worried what my grandmother would do with the information. Grandma Grant wasn't one for subtlety, and I thought she might confront the Mayor with the information as soon as she found out.

I knew I should really tell Chief Wickham and Deputy McGrady what I'd unearthed before I told Grandma Grant.

Besides, I was going to see Grandma Grant at the town hall tonight at the meeting about the resort, so I'd be able to fill her in along with Jess.

I had half expected Yvonne to be hovering around the diner

waiting for me, perhaps even ready with a grudging apology, but there was no sign of her.

As soon as I arrived, I caught sight of Loretta sitting in one of the empty booths. There were quite a few people in the diner, and it was already filling up ahead of the lunchtime rush.

I gazed in horror at one of the booths. There was food smeared all over the table and what looked like a portion of hash browns dumped on the floor. I sighed.

Loretta hovered over to me and said, "I'll give you two guesses who made that mess."

I didn't need two guesses. There was only one person in this town who could make so much mess: a small boy called Tommy Breton. He and his mom came in the diner most days, usually for breakfast, but today they'd obviously decided to grace us with their presence a little later than usual. I didn't for one second think Archie would have left the booth in that state all morning. The table looked like a bomb had hit it.

I sighed as I headed to the back room to pick up a clean apron and start on the clear up.

Archie was just coming out of the kitchen. "Did you see the mess?" he growled. "I've never known a child like it. There's not one other child in Abbott Cove that makes as much mess as that boy."

I sighed. At least Archie wasn't the one who had to clear it up. I put my apron on and tied it around my waist. "I guessed it was him from the state of the table," I said. "Are you going to the town meeting tonight?"

Archie shrugged. "I thought I'd go along. If only for the entertainment value. The mayor is talking, and I'm sure your grand-mother will have something to say about that."

"What do you think of him, Archie?"

Archie frowned. "What do you mean?"

"The Mayor, does he strike you as a violent man?"

Archie shook his head. "I've never really thought about it. I would have said no, but…"

"What?"

"Well, he did look like he was pretty close to getting violent the other day when your grandmother was on the hood of his car."

Fair point, but Grandma Grant had the ability to drive most people to want to commit a violent act.

I nodded, but I still couldn't imagine the Mayor getting so angry he committed murder. He didn't seem the type, but then again, I suppose no one did. Killers didn't come with a warning sign, unfortunately.

I got to work clearing up the table and soon had it looking almost back to normal.

Loretta hovered beside me. Sometimes her constant presence was an irritation. She had been a ghost a long time and was perfectly capable of picking things up and moving objects around, so I didn't see why she couldn't lend a hand now and again.

I smiled at the thought of one of the customers seeing a table wipe itself. Or maybe Loretta could throw a piece of hash brown back at Tommy Breton when he dumped it on the floor.

I was feeling angsty. I hadn't had a chance to talk things through with Jess yet. She was my usual sounding board, but I decided Loretta would do on this occasion.

Once I got all the customers settled and served, I popped out to the back room, giving Loretta a surreptitious sign that she should follow me.

"What is it?" Loretta asked, her ghostly eyes sparkling. Life for Loretta was pretty boring in the diner, and she loved it whenever I shared any gossip or news with her.

"I went to Cherry Town this morning," I told Loretta. "I planned to try and find out who the Mayor was meeting there, and I was shocked to find out it was Yvonne. I think they were having an affair."

Loretta pulled a face. "Ew, that's disgusting."

I happened to agree with her, but I was hoping for a little more input than that.

"Grandma Grant thought he was going to Cherry Town for meetings and taking payments as favors to pass things through the planning committee quickly for the new resort, but actually, he was there to meet up with Yvonne and…"

Loretta's eyes opened wide, and she stared at me before her body started to shake with laughter.

"Oh, it's too ridiculous. Haughty old Yvonne with Mayor Briggs! I can't wait to see her and tease her about it."

I didn't think she was ever going to stop howling with laughter.

I tried to shush her, but it didn't do any good. I suppose it didn't really matter because nobody else could hear her. I had hoped for a little bit of advice, though.

"Loretta, stop laughing," I ordered eventually. "I need your help. If Mayor Briggs was having an affair with Yvonne, do you think it's possible he might have had her killed? After all, he is married. Perhaps he needed to keep the affair quiet, and he thought Yvonne was going to tell someone."

Loretta stopped laughing and shook her head. "I wouldn't have thought he had it in him. Although I have to admit, I never liked him. His eyes are too close together."

"What?" I shook my head. "What does that have to do with it? For goodness sake, you sound just like Grandma Grant."

I gave up on Loretta and left her in the back room. So much for acting as a sounding board. All I learned from Loretta was that the Mayor's eyes were too close together. Useful.

A couple of other customers had entered the diner while I was talking to Loretta, so I quickly took their orders, passed the order slips through the hatch to Archie, and then joined him in the kitchen and started to make a new batch of lemonade.

"The Chief and Joe were in earlier, for breakfast. Joe asked about you," Archie said giving me a pointed look, which I ignored.

"Did they mention the investigation?" I asked.

Archie sighed. "It doesn't sound like they're getting very far. Poor Yvonne. She was snatched from us too soon. I hate to think of her killer getting away with it."

"These things take time. I bet the chief and Joe have plenty of leads we don't know about. I'm sure her killer will be brought to justice, Archie."

He smiled at me and nodded. "I suppose you're right."

For the rest of the day, the diner was pretty busy. I was starting to feel a little nervous that I hadn't seen Yvonne all day. After our fight this morning, I guessed she was trying to punish me.

I stayed a little later after my shift to help Archie clear up because Alice, who was supposed to be taking over from us, was running late.

Archie and I arrived at the town hall for the meeting just in time. Mrs. Townsend shut the doors behind me. I turned to look at the rows of people in attendance. It looked like the whole of Abbot Cove had turned out for this.

Archie slipped into a seat in the back row, and I caught sight of Grandma Grant and Jess sitting near the front and saw that they had saved me a seat.

I wound my way between the chairs, putting up with moans and impatient huffs of breath as I tripped over people's feet to get to my seat.

The mayor was already standing at the front of the room next to a microphone.

I sat down beside Grandma Grant.

"This is going to be good," Grandma said.

Before I had a chance to reply, Mayor Briggs began to talk.

I'd been reflecting on the subject of his affair with Yvonne all day, and I wasn't seeing him in a very favorable light right now.

"Of course, we are all gathered here today to talk about the new resort planned for Abbott Cove, but I must take a moment to mention the recent tragic death in our community," the mayor began and then broke off to dab at his eyes with a handkerchief.

Were they crocodile tears? How could he stand up there in

public and talk about Yvonne as though she were just a casual acquaintance?

"Now, there's been a lot of ruckus recently caused by a certain individual in Abbott Cove." The mayor's tears suddenly dried up as he stared daggers at Grandma Grant. "You would think a long-term Abbott Cove resident would show a little decorum in the face of such a tragic death, and not go to great lengths to draw attention to themselves, throwing tantrums like a child."

I sensed Grandma Grant tense beside me and knew she wanted to respond. Given half a chance, she would be up there bashing him over the head with the microphone.

She wasn't the only one. I was furious on her behalf, especially considering what I now knew.

Mayor Briggs was a class A hypocrite.

Grandma Grant had been right about one thing. He was a cheater, and I wasn't going to sit there and hear him run my grandmother into the ground.

I didn't really think it through. Perhaps if I had, I wouldn't have acted so hastily, but I shot up from my chair and said, "That's quite enough of that, thank you, Mr. Mayor. I'm afraid the games up. I know your little secret."

The mayor stared at me, slack-jawed. His gaze moved between my grandmother and me.

I could hear Jess hissing beside me, "Harper, what are you doing? Sit down!"

Everyone in the hall was staring at me, and I started to feel nervous. I should have waited and confronted him in private, but it was too late to worry about that. I couldn't stop now.

"I went to Cherry Town today," I continued, "and I found out that my grandmother has been right all along. You were conducting secret meetings there."

The mayor's lower lip began to wobble, and he looked around the room in a panic.

The mayor's wife, who was sitting in the front row, turned around to tell me sharply to sit down.

"Don't you dare sit down, Harper," Grandma Grant ordered. "Carry on. I want to hear this."

Grandma Grant obviously still thought this was all about the mayor's dodgy financial deals. She had no idea he'd been having an affair with Yvonne.

I tried to sound more confident than I felt. I put my hands on my hips as I said, "I could tell everyone about it now, including your wife, but I think it would be better coming from you."

To my shock, the mayor started to cry. Not just a steady trickle of tears but full on, body-wracking sobs.

I didn't know where to look or what to do.

But I didn't have to do anything, the floodgates had opened, and the mayor began to admit everything. "You're right. I'm so ashamed. I took money from businesses trying to ingratiate themselves with the resort. People wanted to clear planning faster, and they gave me money to expedite the process. I'm sorry…"

Mayor Briggs turned to look at his wife, and the shock on her face told me she had known absolutely nothing about this.

But she wasn't half as shocked as I was. That wasn't what I'd expected him to say. I'd been expecting him to come clean about his affair.

"What about Yvonne Dean?" I demanded.

The mayor sniffed and wiped his eyes. "Yes, Yvonne was one of the people I took money from. She wanted to have a place in the new resort for her yoga studio."

I looked around at the shocked faces in the audience, and when my gaze settled on Grandma Grant, I saw she was beaming up at me.

She slapped me on the back. "Well done, Harper!"

CHAPTER 16

I FELT LIKE A COMPLETE IDIOT.

I stood in the center of the town hall with Grandma Grant and Jess beside me. People kept walking up and trying to shake my hand, telling me they'd suspected the mayor was suspicious all along.

Hindsight was a wonderful thing.

Despite what everyone was saying now, Grandma Grant was the only one who called it, and now she was bathing in the glow of everyone's admiration, although, undeservedly, most of the attention seemed to be focused on me.

Mayor Briggs had been sent home in disgrace, pending an investigation.

But nobody wanted to go home. Scandals like this didn't often happen in Abbott Cove, and everybody wanted to talk about it and dissect what had happened. Every resident of Abbott Cove had an anecdote about how they knew the mayor was corrupt, and they were just waiting for the day when he was exposed.

The only ones who didn't look too happy were Chief Wickham and Deputy McGrady.

I gulped as I saw them approaching through the crowds of people.

I hadn't even noticed them when I entered the town hall, but I supposed it wasn't surprising. I'd arrived late and had only been looking out for Grandma Grant and Jess.

Joe reached me first. "It looks like you're the town hero again, Harper."

He didn't look happy. Before I replied to Joe, my gaze shifted to Chief Wickham, who looked extremely serious as well.

I should have told the chief and Joe what I'd found out before revealing it dramatically at the town hall. I hadn't planned on doing it, but the mayor annoyed me when he'd made mean comments about Grandma Grant. I had blurted it out in the heat of the moment, and now, I was going to have to apologize.

Before the chief could tell me off, Grandma Grant smiled broadly at him and said, "I told you he was crooked. You should have listened to me, shouldn't you?"

Grandma Grant had never been magnanimous in victory. She was right, and therefore, she was going to make the most of it and rub it in. For how long was anyone's guess. But I thought she would probably dine out on this story until at least Christmas.

"I can't comment on that until after the investigation," Chief Wickham said in a cool tone.

"Don't give me that rubbish about a namby-pamby investigation," Grandma Grant said rudely. "I was right, and nobody believed me. Now you all look like fools."

Like I said, definitely not magnanimous in victory.

I thought I'd better cut in before Grandma Grant made matters even worse.

"I'm very sorry," I said. "I should have come to you and Deputy McGrady before I opened my mouth like that. But he really made me mad with his comments about Grandma Grant. I know she can be a pain but…"

Grandma Grant dug me in the ribs. "Hey!"

"But you have to admit she was right about him." I rubbed my bruised ribs and glared at Grandma Grant.

"I have a question," I said and moved a little closer to Chief Wickham and hoped nobody else would overhear our conversation. "Do you think the mayor could have killed Yvonne?"

Chief Wickham pulled back in surprise, and Joe, who had also heard my comment, frowned. "I doubt it, Harper. Why would you think that?"

I shook my head. If I was honest, I didn't really think the mayor was capable of killing Yvonne, the trouble was, I didn't know anybody who was, and unless we found her killer, Yvonne was destined to remain a ghost and a thorn in my side.

I shrugged. "I don't really. It was just because he was taking bribes from her… I thought perhaps he didn't want her to reveal his secret?"

I was clutching at straws, and I knew it.

Chief Wickham shook his head. "I think that might be a bit of a stretch of logic, Harper. But I promise you we are going to have a very close look at the mayor's affairs, and if he was involved, we'll find out."

I nodded. I had to be satisfied with that.

"So how is the investigation into Yvonne's murder going? Have you got any suspects?"

"I have to hand it to you, Harper," Joe McGrady said dryly. "You're certainly persistent."

* * *

WE FINALLY MANAGED to escape from the hordes of people trying to congratulate us, and we walked Grandma Grant home before Jess and I returned to the cottage.

"What's wrong with you?" Jess asked. "I thought you would be on cloud nine after your dramatic unveiling of the mayor as a dastardly criminal."

Jess's words were sarcastic, but I could see the concern in her eyes and knew it was because I'd been so quiet during the walk home.

I couldn't believe I'd gotten it so wrong.

I knew I could confide in my sister, though. I might worry about what the rest of the town thought of me, but I knew Jess loved me regardless, even when I made a fool of myself.

"I didn't know the mayor was taking money. Grandma Grant should take all the credit for that. I actually thought he'd been having an affair with Yvonne. That's why I confronted him at the town hall."

Jess stopped in her tracks as we walked through the door to the cottage, making me bump into her.

"Ow, what did you stop for?" I asked, rubbing my forehead. I'd cracked it against the back of her head.

"You thought Yvonne was having an affair with Mayor Briggs?" Jess turned around and looked at me in disbelief.

I nodded. I suppose it did seem a bit ridiculous now, but the evidence had seemed very persuasive at the time.

"I had a big argument with Yvonne before I left this morning. She was acting strange, really shifty, and she didn't want me to go to Cherry Town to ask about the mayor. When I went anyway, and the server identified Yvonne as the woman who'd been meeting the mayor, I put two and two together and came up with five." I sighed. "It's all right. You can say it. I'm an idiot."

Jess smiled and ruffled my hair as she threw her keys down on the kitchen counter.

"You're not an idiot, Harper. But I will say you were very lucky that the Mayor confessed to his dodgy financial deals before you'd accused him of having an affair with Yvonne."

I nodded. I supposed I should be thankful for small mercies.

Jess filled up the kettle. "Tea?"

I nodded. I could really do with a cup of chamomile tea this evening. I would need all the help I could get to help me sleep tonight.

"So, I suppose it all makes sense now," Jess said. "You were wondering why Yvonne had picked Abbott Cove as her base, and it was obviously because she was planning to do a deal with the new resort. If she got in with that chain, she could have had yoga classes all around the world in all of their resorts."

I nodded. At least something was making sense. I knew now what Yvonne had been hiding. She was ashamed I would find out about her paying the mayor off in order to secure a contract with the new resort. But that didn't get us any closer to discovering Yvonne's killer.

"I hate to say it," I muttered, "but I actually wish Yvonne was here now. I'm starting to get worried."

Jess lifted the kettle and poured hot water over the dried chamomile.

"Try not to worry, Harper. I'm sure she's somewhere safe, cooling off. Did you accuse her of having an affair?"

I shook my head. "No, thankfully. I didn't come up with that theory until after we'd had the argument."

Jess smiled as she handed me a cup of tea. "No harm done then."

"Thanks. I still feel guilty, though."

"She did lie to you, Harper. Perhaps not in the way you thought, but she was paying the mayor to bypass regulations. Money is a powerful motivator."

I nodded sadly. It did make sense. Yvonne had never been interested in Abbott Cove. It wasn't the town she was interested in, but the resort.

We drank tea and chatted for a while and then Jess went to bed.

I didn't feel a bit sleepy. I wasn't sure I'd be able to get any sleep, knowing that Yvonne was roaming the countryside somewhere. Maybe I had been a little harsh...

After Jess had gone to bed, feeling sorry for myself, I wandered out onto the porch, keeping an eye out for the little cat. I'd taken to calling it Smudge in my head, named for the little smudge of white by its nose. But there was no sign of the cat. I sighed. Even the cat had given up on me.

I'd been kidding myself. How could I help Yvonne get justice? I'd gotten the business with the mayor completely wrong.

Brooding on my mistakes, I locked up and went to bed. If Yvonne came back, I didn't have to worry about leaving the door open. She could float right through it.

I lay awake for ages. The chamomile tea obviously hadn't done the trick.

I couldn't help stressing over Yvonne, and worrying how angry the chief and Joe were with me for not telling them about the mayor before my dramatic revelation.

It was after midnight when with a sigh I admitted defeat. I wasn't going to be able to get to sleep, so I slipped out of bed and grabbed the large book of spells from the top of my dresser.

I took it back to bed with me, propped it up on my knees and opened it.

It worked a treat. By page three, I was out for the count.

CHAPTER 17

THE FOLLOWING MORNING, there was still no sign of Yvonne. I was starting to feel rather despondent and a little worried.

When I arrived at the diner to start the early shift, I felt my stomach twist when I realized Yvonne was not here either. I was sure nothing terrible could have happened to her, but I was worried about her mental state. No one else in Abbott Cove could see her now that she was a ghost, and she must have felt isolated. She had been through an awful experience, and I should have been more understanding when I had the chance.

I didn't have time to dwell on the fact Yvonne was missing for long, though. Loretta was in a tizzy. She swooped around me as I hung up my coat in the back room, turning in circles so fast it made me feel dizzy.

"I take it there's no sign of Yvonne, then?" I asked Loretta.

"Forget Yvonne! I have news!"

I plucked a clean apron from the peg and raised an eyebrow at Loretta. She was clearly bursting to share her news with me.

I have to say I wasn't very excited. The last time Loretta had been like this, it turned out she just wanted to tell me that Archie had swapped the supplier for the bacon delivery.

"Go on, tell me quickly. I've got to get to work."

Loretta chuckled, pleased with herself. "You just missed a mysterious stranger, who came to the diner asking about Yvonne and Carol."

I shouldn't have doubted her. This was much more exciting news than Archie changing bacon suppliers.

I opened my mouth to ask a question, but I didn't get a chance before Loretta continued, "He was ever so handsome. Dashing, in my opinion. Archie told him that Carol and Louise were staying at The Oceanview Guesthouse, so I think that's where he's gone now."

Loretta looked terribly pleased with herself, and my curiosity was piqued.

"Who was he? What was his name?"

Loretta's beaming smile shrank noticeably. "I didn't catch his name. He was already talking to Archie by the time I'd noticed him."

That didn't matter. I could ask Archie about him. I began to move towards the kitchen and then turned and said over my shoulder, "How did he know Yvonne and Carol?"

Loretta gave a little huff. Obviously, she wasn't pleased with my reaction to her news. "I can't tell you everything. You may not have noticed, Harper. But I can't actually ask people questions anymore, since I am a ghost!"

Loretta folded her arms over her chest and hovered round in a circle so she could turn her back to me.

I paused by the door and then turned around, walking back over to Loretta and stepping in front of her so I could look her in the eye.

"I'm sorry, Loretta. That is very interesting news. I think it's an important development. Well done."

Loretta loved to be complimented, and I could see the frosty mood thaw from her eyes.

"That's okay," she said, smiling again. "I knew you'd be interested. That's why I listened in on his conversation with Archie."

I grinned at her, thanked her again and then went off to the kitchen to find Archie.

I had to find out who this mysterious stranger was.

Archie was whistling to himself as he was frying up eggs.

"Good morning, Archie. How are you?"

I was determined to act casual and wait for him to bring up the news of this mysterious stranger. After all, I couldn't very well tell him my source of information was a ghost who lived in his diner.

Archie turned around and gave me a brief smile before turning his attention back to the pan of eggs. "Not too bad," he said. "But I am looking forward to Sarah getting back next week. All these extra shifts and working in the kitchen have really taken it out of me."

I began to set up a new batch of coffee for the coffee machine.

"Oh, I'd love one," Archie said, hinting, even though I always made him a coffee when I got in. He didn't need to ask. It was one of our daily rituals.

I grinned at him. "Sure thing."

I entered the diner and made my way to the coffee machine, which was set up by the counter.

Old Bob already had a cup of coffee and was waiting anxiously for his normal breakfast of eggs and extra-crispy bacon.

There was nobody else in the diner, so I poured Archie and me a cup of coffee and carried them back through to the kitchen.

"Here you go," I said cheerfully, putting the cup of coffee down on the stainless steel counter.

I lingered in the kitchen, eager to give him the opportunity to tell me about the man who'd called into the diner not long before I'd arrived.

I wished I'd turned up a little earlier so I could have seen the mystery man for myself.

Archie gave me a sideways glance. "Don't you have tables to clean?"

I groaned. There were only two tables waiting to be cleared. They could wait. I was far more interested in what Archie could tell me about this stranger. But Archie didn't appear to be in a very talkative mood this morning.

He needed prompting, and I wasn't very good at that. It needed a light touch, tact and subtlety, and I was afraid I took after

Grandma Grant on that score. I had as much subtlety as a sledgehammer.

Still, I tried my best.

"So, did anything out of the ordinary happen this morning before I got here?"

Archie used the spatula to flip the eggs and then looked at me with a puzzled frown on his face. "What are you talking about, Harper?"

"I'm just making conversation," I said defensively.

"Well, there's a time and a place for conversation, and it's when you've finished clearing off the tables."

Frustrated, I walked back through to the diner to do what Archie had asked me.

On a usual day, I would have cleaned the tables straightaway, but I was dying to find out who this mysterious man was. I couldn't believe Archie hadn't told me as soon as I'd walked in. We had plenty of tourists in Abbott Cove, but Archie knew this man wasn't a tourist. He was connected to Yvonne. Archie loved a little gossip, so I'd expected him to blurt out everything that had happened as soon as I arrived.

But I hadn't given up. I cleaned the tables as fast as I could and then carried the plates back into the kitchen to load up the dishwasher.

Now it was time for attempt number two.

"I thought I saw somebody coming out of the diner earlier," I lied. "He didn't look like a regular. Was he a tourist?"

Archie was now humming away to himself, plating up Old Bob's eggs.

"Sorry, what was that, Harper?" Archie said as he handed me the plate to give Old Bob.

"Never mind," I muttered and took the plate.

I was so desperate for information about this mysterious stranger I almost asked Old Bob if he'd overheard anything, but I doubted he would be able to tell me much. Old Bob was not the talkative type.

He nodded his thanks as I put down his plate of eggs and began methodically to demolish them, pausing only for sips of his black coffee.

I was starting to get annoyed now. After all, Abbott Cove was a small town where everyone knew each other's business. What's the point in living in a small town if you didn't get to hear the gossip?

I marched back into the kitchen, determined to get it out of Archie one way or another.

"Who was the stranger who turned up earlier asking for Yvonne and Carol?"

Archie looked up. "How did you know about that?"

I shrugged. I'd already fibbed once this morning. Would one more fib really hurt?

"Old Bob told me."

"Oh, right. He said his name was Brian Constantine. Apparently, he used to be Yvonne's business partner."

Archie paused to wipe down the worktops and then picked up

his coffee to take it through into the diner because he didn't like to eat or drink anything in the kitchen.

I picked up my coffee and followed him.

"Brian Constantine," I muttered. "It was strange Yvonne didn't mention him."

I hadn't realized I'd spoken those words aloud until Archie looked at me sharply and said, "Well, why would she? It's not as if she knew you very well, and I have to say, Harper, you weren't always very friendly towards her."

I bit back my response. Just because I hadn't fawned all over Yvonne, didn't mean I wasn't friendly. Although Archie was right. Her prickly nature had put me off right from the start. But of course, Archie didn't know how much time I'd spent with Yvonne after she died and became a ghost.

I was starting to realize just how much Yvonne had been holding back from me. Firstly, she'd been hiding the fact she'd been bribing the Mayor, and now I'd found out she had a business partner she hadn't bothered to mention. There were all kinds of possible motives that could be tied to a business partner.

"He was a rather surly character," Archie said before taking a sip of his coffee.

He could have been a charming man, and Archie would still have said that. He wouldn't believe anyone was good enough for Yvonne.

"Maybe I should go and talk to him," I suggested. "I could go to the guesthouse and…"

Archie shook his head firmly. "Not a chance. It's only you and me this morning, and we need all hands on deck."

I felt a bubble of panic build up inside me. What if Brian Constantine left town after speaking to Louise and Carol? He could be our only suspect.

"But Archie, what if he was involved in Yvonne's murder," I whispered, even though our only customer was Old Bob, who was far too busy concentrating on his eggs to listen to us.

Archie puffed out his cheeks as he exhaled a long breath. "Harper, it's none of our business. I'm sure the chief and Deputy McGrady will be questioning him in due course."

Archie trusted the law enforcement in Abbott Cove, which was odd because after the last murder in Abbott Cove, Deputy McGrady and the chief had considered Archie a suspect.

I looked longingly at the door, but Archie shook his head again, and I knew it was hopeless. I would have to hope that the chief and Joe McGrady had learned of this mysterious stranger.

"Perhaps I could call the chief and tell him about Yvonne's business partner."

"There's no need. Deputy McGrady called in to pick up coffee and muffins this morning. He spoke to Brian and made arrangements to speak to him later today."

I nodded. There wasn't much else I could do. I may not have been able to talk to Brian Constantine, but at least the chief and Deputy McGrady would.

CHAPTER 18

My luck changed right around lunchtime.

"There he is," screeched Loretta as the bell above the door chimed, and the tall, dark, handsome stranger, Brian Constantine, walked into the diner. He was followed by Deputy Joe McGrady and Chief Wickham. I guessed they'd been talking to him and then brought him here for lunch. Abbott Cove's law enforcement officers were nothing if not hospitable.

Loretta had been right. Brian Constantine was dashing. There was no other word for it. He looked like he belonged on the cover of a magazine. His dark hair was slicked back and slightly too long. His skin was tanned and smooth, and he had high cheekbones and smoldering brown eyes.

All three men took a seat, and Joe and the chief waved their hellos to the other customers in the diner.

"I told you he was handsome," Loretta said as we both stared at Brian Constantine.

I nodded. "He's gorgeous," I muttered as I walked toward their table.

Joe looked up sharply and frowned at me.

I blinked and came to my senses. Darn it. I needed to be more careful. What was wrong with me?

I smiled and asked to take their orders.

The Chief and Brian Constantine asked for lemonade, but Joe ordered coffee.

I brought them their drinks and tried to pick up a little of their conversation, but annoyingly, they paused when I came to the table with the tray and didn't continue talking until I left again.

I wished Yvonne was here, so I could at least ask her about Brian. I knew absolutely nothing about him.

While I was stacking the trays under the counter, Joe got up from the table and walked across to me. He downed his hot coffee in two gulps and held out the cup for me.

"Could I get a refill, please, Harper?"

I was a little taken aback at how quickly he'd finished his coffee. He was obviously a man in need of caffeine.

"Sure," I said taking the cup from him and taking it over to the coffee machine.

Over my shoulder, I said, "So, who is the mystery man?"

I thought I'd asked the question casually, but Joe's tone was cold when he replied, "You mean the gorgeous mystery man?"

I flushed.

Darn it. He had heard me.

I grinned and shrugged. There was no point in pretending. I said, "I'm only human."

Joe frowned. "He's Brian Constantine, Yvonne's old business partner." Joe turned back to look at the table where Brian Constantine was deep in conversation with Chief Wickham. "We asked him to come down to the station and answer a few questions. The Chief invited him to lunch, but I don't like him."

Interesting. I wondered if he could be a potential suspect.

"Why not? Do you think he killed Yvonne?"

"Keep your voice down, Harper." Joe took the cup of coffee I held out to him.

"He doesn't look like a murderer," I mused, trying to imagine those nicely manicured hands tightening Yvonne's scarf around her neck to throttle her.

I shivered.

"There's more to people than how they look, Harper," Joe said.

"I'm perfectly aware of that, thanks." I narrowed my eyes. "Besides, Deputy McGrady, I'm sure your looks have helped you to get out of a tight spot on more than one occasion."

"My looks?" His mouth quirked upwards in a smile. "Is that a compliment?"

I shrugged. He could take it any way he wanted. He was trying to flirt with me; I was sure of it. But it hadn't come to anything last time. It was probably something he did to pass the time, and I wasn't prepared to fall for a player.

I started to turn away, but before I did my gaze flickered over his face. There was no denying that Deputy McGrady did have gorgeous eyes and...

I mentally shook myself.

Snap out of it, Harper. Concentrate.

* * *

HALF AN HOUR LATER, the chief and Joe left Brian Constantine in the diner, reading the Abbott Cove Gazette.

I'd served all the other tables and now hovered beside the counter deciding how to proceed. What I really wanted to do was go over, introduce myself and try to get Brian talking. But it was hard to go up and talk to somebody I didn't know. What if he thought I was just being a nosy gossip?

Finally, I took a deep breath and headed over to the table. I needed to take a chance. It could be my only opportunity to talk to him if he left town this afternoon.

I slipped into the opposite side of the booth without waiting for an invitation.

"Hello, I'm Harper," I said brightly, giving him my most dazzling smile.

Brian seemed rather shocked and sat back abruptly in his seat.

He hesitated for a moment before folding the newspaper and saying, "I'm Brian."

I nodded. "I know. You were Yvonne's business partner. I was very upset to hear about Yvonne. Were you very close?"

If Brian was puzzled by my sudden line of questioning, he hid it well and smiled charmingly at me. "We were. We'd been business partners for a number of years, and I only just learned of her death yesterday. It was such a tragedy."

I gave him a sympathetic smile.

Now that I was up close, I could see him more clearly. He was certainly good-looking, but his eyes were a little too close together... Oh no, now I sounded like Grandma Grant and Loretta. Their craziness was rubbing off on me.

"Have you been to see Carol yet?" I asked. "She's been ever so upset."

Brian nodded. "I imagine she would be. She was very close to her sister. I haven't been yet, but your colleague, the one I spoke to earlier, told me they were staying at The Oceanview Guesthouse."

I nodded. "That's right. It's just down on the harbor front. It's a lovely little guesthouse, but I don't suppose Carol is really in the mood to enjoy it at the moment. Louise is still there, too. She was Yvonne's personal assistant. Did you know her?"

Brian suddenly seemed evasive. A frown flickered across his face and then he said, "Oh, not really. I may have met her once or twice."

I nodded and opened my mouth to ask another question, but he cut me off, "If you'll excuse me, I think it's time I went to the guesthouse now."

He stood up and tucked the paper under his arm. I watched him stride toward the exit.

I wasn't sure about Brian Constantine. There was something not quite right about him. He reached the door and then turned around to look back at me. When he saw I was still watching him, he gave me a brief smile and opened the door.

As he did so, Yvonne zoomed in floating right through him. Brian didn't even blink.

"What is he doing here? That rat!" Yvonne exclaimed as she sped into the diner and floated up to me.

I couldn't exactly answer Yvonne in the diner full of customers, and as I looked around, I saw that there were a couple of people who needed top ups for their drinks. I tried to signal to Yvonne discretely, indicating with a nod of my head she should go into the back room. I was planning to go and talk to her as soon as I could.

Yvonne went off muttering away to herself, "Of all the low down, dirty, backstabbing…"

I quickly dealt with the customers, making sure everyone was all right and then nipped into the back room.

I was so glad to see that Yvonne was still okay. I had been worried about her.

"Why didn't you tell me about Brian Constantine?" I demanded as soon as I shut the door behind us.

"Well, that's a lovely welcome back," Yvonne said sarcastically. "Hello, Yvonne, how lovely to see you. How have you been?"

I rolled my eyes. "I'm glad you're back. I'm sorry we argued, but we're on the same team."

"That is hardly what I would call an apology, Harper."

Despite the fact I'd been regretting my harsh words since Yvonne had disappeared, I felt my anger bubble to the surface again. Why should I apologize? After all, she was the one who'd lied to me.

I tilted my head to the side and gave Yvonne a knowing look. "I found out about you and the Mayor."

Yvonne sheepishly avoided eye contact. "I would have told you, but it wasn't relevant."

"How do you know? Something like that could be relevant. And now I've found out you have a business partner, whom you obviously don't like very much. Why didn't you tell me about him?"

"I haven't seen Brian for months. I cut him out of the business. He never did any work. He just sat back and enjoyed the profits."

"So he was lazy, but is there any reason he would be angry enough to kill you?"

Yvonne scoffed. "I very much doubt he would have it in him. He's not someone who likes hard work. He prefers to cozy up to a successful woman, who is too silly to see through him so she can do all the hard work for him while he benefits from the profits."

I raised an eyebrow, and Yvonne seemed to realize she was the silly woman in this scenario, so she hurriedly rushed on and changed the subject. "I suppose he was a little sour about the fact he was going to miss out on the resort deal."

I nodded. That was interesting. I turned to Yvonne, "It looks as though we could have a suspect."

I couldn't talk to Yvonne for as long as I would have liked because I had a diner full of customers, so I left her in the back room, promising her we would have a long talk tonight, and went to finish my shift.

The afternoon shift seemed to drag on forever.

When I said goodbye to Archie, I was surprised at how tired he looked, he wasn't that much older than me, although I always thought of him as some kind of father figure.

I think we were both looking forward to Sarah getting back and easing our workloads.

I walked along Main Street with Yvonne hovering beside me. We didn't talk until we left the residential area.

When we stepped onto the woodland trail and were out of sight, I said, "So, tell me more about Brian."

"There's not much to say," Yvonne said. "I got fed up with him. I realized I was doing all the work, and he was taking all the profits, so I dumped him. That would have been that, but then he tried to manipulate Carol, and that was just cruel. He bought her flowers and asked her out on a date." Yvonne shook her head and pursed her lips. "Of course, I forbade it. He was using her to get to me, and I wasn't going to stand for it."

The way I saw it, there were two possible reasons Brian could have been angry enough with Yvonne to kill her. Firstly, she had chucked him out of the business, and secondly, she had ruined his romantic chances with her sister, Carol.

I turned to look at Yvonne and asked, "Was he very angry?"

Yvonne shrugged. "I suppose he was. But I didn't care. I wasn't going to let him make a fool of my sister."

"Could he have been angry enough to kill?"

Yvonne hesitated before replying. "I suppose. I wish I could remember that night in the cabin, but I can't remember anything."

We were getting towards the end of the trail now, and I shivered. I was wearing a cardigan. I hadn't brought my jacket, and the evening had turned chilly.

"Where did you get to anyway? I was worried about you?"

"You needn't have been," Yvonne said. "After all, you were the one who said I couldn't get hurt since I was already a ghost."

I gave Yvonne a sideways glance. "I'm sorry. Can we put all that unpleasantness behind us?"

Yvonne nodded. "Yes, I suppose so. I should have told you about the payments I'd made to the Mayor. I'm sorry."

That took me by surprise – Yvonne Dean had actually apologized to me.

"So where were you? Did you stay in town?"

Yvonne smiled, and her eyes gleamed as she said, "I've been investigating."

I turned to her, surprised. "Investigating? On your own?"

Yvonne nodded. "Yes, I went back to the cabin, and I found a clue."

I grinned. This was very good news.

"Of course, I couldn't actually pick it up. Loretta makes it look easy, but I haven't yet learned how to pick objects up. Anyway, I found some fabric on the window frame. My working theory is that the killer strangled me, locked the door and then climbed out of the window to get away, but their clothing got caught on a piece of wood."

Her eyes sparkled with excitement as she told me her theory.

"Um, was the fabric you found wool by any chance?"

Yvonne nodded, a puzzled frown creasing her forehead.

"Was it cream colored?"

Yvonne was really looking confused now. "Yes, how did you know that?"

I pulled an apologetic expression. "I'm afraid that's mine. I looked in the window the morning we found your body, and I caught my sweater on a splinter of wood on the way down. Sorry. It was really Mrs. Townsend's fault. She forgot she was supposed to be supporting me."

All the excitement and enthusiasm seemed to drain out of Yvonne, and I felt bad to be the one to disappoint her.

"I suppose it's back to the drawing board then," she said morosely.

CHAPTER 19

WHEN YVONNE and I got back to the cottage, I was surprised to see that Jess was waiting for us.

As I walked in, I saw a number of items placed on the table and a feeling of dread overtook me.

"What's all this?" I asked nervously.

Jess grinned. "I'm going to help you learn your spells and potions."

I smothered a groan. Jess meant well, but I knew I was never going to be good at casting spells. It would be easier all round if everybody just accepted that.

"I don't know Jess. I've had such a busy day and –"

"No excuses," Jess said firmly, brushing her hands together and then pointing at the items on the table.

"We're going to make a potion."

That perked Yvonne up. Her mood changed in an instant. A moment ago, she'd been maudlin and depressed because I told her the clue she'd found was actually a fragment of my sweater. Now, she was practically buzzing with excitement.

"I've never seen someone perform a genuine spell before," she said. "Oh, it's so exciting."

I rolled my eyes and looked at her. "I wouldn't get too excited. It is me we're talking about. I'll probably find a way to mess it up."

Jess, who had seen me turn my head and address thin air, realized Yvonne was back.

"I take it Yvonne has returned. Is she okay?"

I moved across to the table and nodded. "Yes, she's been trying to do a little investigating herself, but it didn't work out too well. We did have a visit from Brian Constantine at the diner today, though. He was Yvonne's old business manager, and there was some bad feeling between them."

Jess cocked an eyebrow. "Do you think he did it?"

"I'm not sure. There is something about him that seems a bit suspicious to me, but I can't quite put my finger on it."

"What does Yvonne think?" Jess asked.

I turned to Yvonne, and she sneered. "I still don't think he would have the gumption to do something like that." She sighed. "I just wish I could remember something about that night."

I turned to Jess and said, "Yvonne is convinced he couldn't have killed her, but the chief and Deputy McGrady are checking him out and looking into his background."

"That's good," Jess said. "Now, let's get down to business."

I sat down at the table nervously, looking at the dried herbs and liquids in front of me. "What do I have to do?"

Jess picked up the large book of spells from where I'd left it on the cabinet and brought it over to the dining table. She opened it and pointed to a spell.

"I thought this would be an appropriate choice. We are going to make a happy potion."

I had to admit a happy potion was appealing. I could do with being cheered up a bit. It was easy to start feeling defeated when you were looking for a killer and had no idea where to start.

"Right," I said, determined to give it my best shot.

I pulled the spell book towards me and read the little introduction. Like most spells, it had a disclaimer. They all did. The title, "Happy Potion," was written in large capital letters, and then in small letters underneath, was the disclaimer: "Caution, potion may not actually make you feel happy."

The trouble with potions and spells was that they were very dependent on the individual. That's what separated a mediocre witch from a good one, or even a terrible witch like me from a mediocre one.

A witch was supposed to make the potion and then chant the spell. You didn't even need to say the spell out loud. As long as a witch thought the words, that was sufficient to send the spell off into the world. According to the book of spells, that was enough to do the trick. I wouldn't know. Every spell I'd ever tried to cast had messed up.

Granted, I hadn't actually tried very hard previously. That was because I was quite lazy and always took the easy way out. I knew my own flaws. Spells were hard.

"Let's make a start," Jess said, taking charge. "First of all, you need a list of a few items that make you feel happy. Not memories," Jess warned. "But actual physical things."

I nodded and tried to think about things that made me happy.

I hesitated. It was difficult to be put on the spot. Could I say chocolate?

"Come on, Harper, it's not that hard," Jess said, trying to encourage me. "What is your favorite fruit?" she prompted.

"Strawberries," I answered immediately. That was an easy one.

"Good. And you like the rain, don't you?"

I nodded. I found it relaxing. I loved being warm and cozy inside and watching the rain. Jess and Grandma Grant both thought I was odd.

"Yes, rain, and I like the smell of cut grass and the taste of chocolate."

Yvonne made a tutting sound.

So sue me. I like chocolate.

Jess nodded. Now we had a list of items, and she sent me outside to collect some rainwater from the garden rain tank and a few blades of grass.

While I was doing that, Jess chopped up some strawberries.

When I returned, with Yvonne watching closely, Jess told me to place all the items on an extra-large dock leaf.

"Why is she using a dock leaf?" Yvonne asked.

"I suppose we could do it on a chopping board or a bowl," I said. "It would probably work the same way, but having it on something organic like this maintains a connection with the natural world. It's thought to work better."

Jess instructed me to mix the items together, which I did, and the resulting mixture looked pretty disgusting.

"Excellent," Jess said. "Now you need to anoint us with the mixture and then chant the spell."

I leaned forward and stuck my finger in the churned up strawberry, chocolate, grass and rainwater mixture and grinned as I streaked it across Jess's forehead. I did the same to mine and then went through the motions of pretending to do it to Yvonne, but obviously it didn't work because my fingers just passed right through her. Still, I wanted her to feel included.

Then I took a deep breath and read the spell from the spell book.

Although I didn't need to, I spoke aloud in the steady rhythm that Grandma Grant used to recite spells.

When I'd finished, I put down the spell book and waited expectantly.

"How do you feel?" Jess asked.

I was as surprised as anyone to realize I did feel better, a lot more positive, in fact.

"I feel pretty good," I said, smiling at Jess.

She beamed back at me. "See, Harper. I knew you could do it! It just takes a little effort and some practice."

I was starting to think that Jess was right. Maybe this spells and potions lark wasn't as hard as I thought it was going to be.

But before I could get too pleased with myself, I heard Yvonne mutter beside me, "Well, it didn't work on me. I still feel depressed."

* * *

THE FOLLOWING MORNING, I was back at the diner for the early shift. I was in a pretty good mood after my successful spell casting last night, but Yvonne was still moping, and I couldn't really blame her. We were no closer to finding her killer. I could only hope that Joe and the chief were closing in on a suspect. Right now, the only suspect I could think of who had any merit was Yvonne's ex-business partner, Brian Constantine.

When Yvonne and I entered the back room of the diner, Loretta immediately joined us by floating through the wall. She appeared to be in an even more excitable mood than the other day.

"You should have been here last night," Loretta said. "Brian and Louise were here together."

I shrugged off my jacket and frowned. "Brian and Louise? I thought Brian had been interested in Carol, not Louise."

I turned to Yvonne to see what she thought of this news.

She looked pensive and confused as though the news puzzled her as much as it did me. I had a feeling we were missing a piece of the jigsaw, and even Yvonne didn't know the full story.

"Do you think you could have got it wrong? Maybe there was something going on between Brian and Louise rather than Brian and your sister?" I asked Yvonne.

Yvonne shook her head slowly. "No, I don't think so."

Loretta was annoyed at the distraction. "You didn't let me finish," she said. "It didn't appear to me like they were enjoying their conversation if you know what I mean."

Loretta waggled her eyebrows suggestively.

"No, I don't know what you mean," I said.

Loretta shook her head as though she was very disappointed in both Yvonne and me. "They weren't getting along well. He was being very demanding, and she was upset."

"What were they talking about?" Yvonne asked.

"Well, I tried my best to eavesdrop, but I couldn't hear their entire conversation. Something about a secret, and he told her she was going to be sorry."

"Sorry? What did he mean by that?" I asked.

Loretta was rapidly losing her patience. "I thought you would be grateful. How am I supposed to know why she's going to be sorry? I just know what he said."

"Oh, I'm sorry, Loretta. Carry on."

"Well, the main thing that got my attention was the fact they were discussing some secret. Obviously, that's very significant."

"Did they mention the murder?" Yvonne asked.

Loretta turned to her with a deadpan expression. "Funnily enough, no, they didn't start to talk about how they killed you when they were sitting in the middle of a busy diner."

I ignored Loretta's sarcasm. I was used to it by now, and it rolled off my back.

"Yvonne, what do you think? Could Brian and Louise have been working together?"

Yvonne shook her head. "Brian is a devious snake, and Louise was a rubbish assistant, but they wouldn't have killed me. For a start, Brian is an opportunist. He waits for other people to act, and then he takes advantage."

Yvonne had known both Brian and Louise a lot better than Loretta and me, so we were forced to rely on her instincts.

But if they weren't referring to Yvonne's murder, then what was the secret they were discussing?

I sighed. There was something about this whole situation that seemed to get more complicated with each passing moment.

"Do you know what secret they were referring to?" Loretta asked Yvonne.

Yvonne hesitated for a moment and then shook her head rapidly. "No, of course, I don't. Why should I?"

Loretta raised a pale, ghostly eyebrow and said, "The lady doth protest too much, methinks."

I had to agree.

Despite the fact I pestered Yvonne for the rest of my shift, she refused to reveal what the secret was. She insisted she didn't have the first idea, but I'd known Yvonne long enough now to realize she was lying.

It was infuriating. I couldn't help thinking how much more progress we could have made if only she'd trusted me from the start. What other things would turn up out of the woodwork from Yvonne's past before we were through?

After work, instead of going directly home, I went to the Lobster Shack to pick up a crochet pattern for Grandma Grant from Betty.

On our way back, with Yvonne chatting inanely on about how Betty could improve her hairstyle, I paused beside the alleyway next to the ice cream parlor.

"It's almost dinnertime," Yvonne said, sounding scandalized. "You can't possibly be thinking about buying an ice cream cone now?"

I put a finger to my lips, not because I was afraid of anyone over-hearing Yvonne as nobody else could hear her nagging, but because I thought I could hear someone else talking.

Voices were coming from the bottom of the alley.

Urgent whispers.

I took a couple of steps along the alley, creeping closer and catching fragments of conversation.

There was a man's voice and a woman's. Both sounded familiar.

It was still daylight, but the alleyway was narrow and didn't get much sun. I stuck to the shadows, my back against the wall.

"Harper, hang on. Be careful," Yvonne said, trying to grab my arm and pull me back. Unfortunately for her, her fingers floated right through me.

There was no way I was leaving now because I'd recognized the voices.

It was Louise and Brian, and they were having a very heated discussion.

Brian's voice was loud and clear, "I'm sure you wouldn't want people to find out."

Even though I couldn't see him from where I stood, I could hear the cold, callous tone in his voice, and it made me shiver.

Louise sounded tearful as she said, "You're a nasty man! It's blackmail. It's against the law."

Brian laughed. "So sue me."

"How did you find out? It was Yvonne, wasn't it? I trusted her. She promised me she wouldn't tell."

"I don't reveal my sources, babe," Brian said, sounding like a bad villain in a B-movie.

I didn't quite catch what they said next because Yvonne was talking right in my ear.

I waved my hand at her, trying to get her to shut up.

Louise muttered something about being unable to afford it, and then Brian growled, "Pay up or…"

And it was at that moment, my cell phone buzzed and began tinkling out a silly ringtone. The "William Tell Overture." Grandma Grant had obviously been messing with my phone.

I gasped in horror as I heard Brian say, "Hey! Who's there?"

I exchanged a panicked look with Yvonne and then ran as fast as I could.

I hadn't run for ages, but the thought of being caught eavesdropping by Brian Constantine was an incredible motivator. There was no way I was going to slow down and let Brian catch me in the alleyway.

Once I passed the white and blue gift store on Main Street, I tried to slow down. All my instincts were driving me to get away as fast as I could, but I knew when Brian exited the alleyway, he would notice if he saw me running.

My best chance to get away without being noticed was to act as though I was merely out for a walk and a bit of window shopping.

"Really, Harper. That was quite impressive. I didn't know you could run like that. You wouldn't think it to look at you," Yvonne's gaze traveled up and down my figure, and I turned to scowl at her.

Yvonne was a master at backhanded compliments.

Usually, I would have ignored Yvonne on Main Street, the chances of running into someone or having someone overhear me was too great, but today I couldn't hold back.

"Do you think Brian realized it was me?"

Yvonne shook her head. "No, I saw him come out of the alley. He definitely heard your phone ring and knew someone was there, but he didn't see you running away."

I let out a long sigh. That had been a close call.

I fished my cell phone out of my pocket. "It didn't ring. It was a message tone," I said. "It's just Grandma Grant asking me where her crochet pattern is. She obviously changed the message alert under her name on my phone. Trust her not to pick something discrete."

Yvonne burst out laughing.

"What's so funny?"

"The sight of you running away to the sound of the "William Tell Overture"! I haven't laughed so hard since I died. The happy spell didn't cheer me up, but that did. Thanks, Harper."

"You're welcome," I said and couldn't help laughing, too. I supposed it must have looked pretty amusing.

We walked quickly along the wooded trail, mainly because I was still spooked and worried Brian might catch up with us.

No matter what Yvonne said, I was still convinced he must have seen me.

CHAPTER 20

DESPITE THE FACT I pestered Yvonne for the rest of my shift, she refused to reveal what the secret was. She insisted she didn't have the first idea, but I'd known Yvonne long enough now to realize she was lying.

It was infuriating. I couldn't help thinking how much more progress we could have made if only she'd trusted me from the start. What other things would turn up out of the woodwork from Yvonne's past before we were through?

After work, instead of going directly home, I went to the Lobster Shack to pick up a crochet pattern for Grandma Grant from Betty.

On our way back, with Yvonne chatting inanely on about how Betty could improve her hairstyle, I paused beside the alleyway next to the ice cream parlor.

"It's almost dinnertime," Yvonne said, sounding scandalized. "You can't possibly be thinking about buying an ice cream cone now?"

I put a finger to my lips, not because I was afraid of anyone over-hearing Yvonne as nobody else could hear her nagging, but because I thought I could hear someone else talking.

Voices were coming from the bottom of the alley.

Urgent whispers.

I took a couple of steps along the alley, creeping closer and catching fragments of conversation.

There was a man's voice and a woman's. Both sounded familiar.

It was still daylight, but the alleyway was narrow and didn't get much sun. I stuck to the shadows, my back against the wall.

"Harper, hang on. Be careful," Yvonne said, trying to grab my arm and pull me back. Unfortunately for her, her fingers floated right through me.

There was no way I was leaving now because I'd recognized the voices.

It was Louise and Brian, and they were having a very heated discussion.

Brian's voice was loud and clear, "I'm sure you wouldn't want people to find out."

Even though I couldn't see him from where I stood, I could hear the cold, callous tone in his voice, and it made me shiver.

Louise sounded tearful as she said, "You're a nasty man! It's blackmail. It's against the law."

Brian laughed. "So sue me."

"How did you find out? It was Yvonne, wasn't it? I trusted her. She promised me she wouldn't tell."

"I don't reveal my sources, babe," Brian said, sounding like a bad villain in a B-movie.

I didn't quite catch what they said next because Yvonne was talking right in my ear.

I waved my hand at her, trying to get her to shut up.

Louise muttered something about being unable to afford it, and then Brian growled, "Pay up or…"

And it was at that moment, my cell phone buzzed and began tinkling out a silly ringtone. The "William Tell Overture." Grandma Grant had obviously been messing with my phone.

I gasped in horror as I heard Brian say, "Hey! Who's there?"

I exchanged a panicked look with Yvonne and then ran as fast as I could.

I hadn't run for ages, but the thought of being caught eavesdropping by Brian Constantine was an incredible motivator. There was no way I was going to slow down and let Brian catch me in the alleyway.

Once I passed the white and blue gift store on Main Street, I tried to slow down. All my instincts were driving me to get away as fast as I could, but I knew when Brian exited the alleyway, he would notice if he saw me running.

My best chance to get away without being noticed was to act as though I was merely out for a walk and a bit of window shopping.

"Really, Harper. That was quite impressive. I didn't know you could run like that. You wouldn't think it to look at you," Yvonne's gaze traveled up and down my figure, and I turned to scowl at her.

Yvonne was a master at backhanded compliments.

Usually, I would have ignored Yvonne on Main Street, the chances of running into someone or having someone overhear me was too great, but today I couldn't hold back.

"Do you think Brian realized it was me?"

Yvonne shook her head. "No, I saw him come out of the alley. He definitely heard your phone ring and knew someone was there, but he didn't see you running away."

I let out a long sigh. That had been a close call.

I fished my cell phone out of my pocket. "It didn't ring. It was a message tone," I said. "It's just Grandma Grant asking me where her crochet pattern is. She obviously changed the message alert under her name on my phone. Trust her not to pick something discrete."

Yvonne burst out laughing.

"What's so funny?"

"The sight of you running away to the sound of the "William Tell Overture"! I haven't laughed so hard since I died. The happy spell didn't cheer me up, but that did. Thanks, Harper."

"You're welcome," I said and couldn't help laughing, too. I supposed it must have looked pretty amusing.

We walked quickly along the wooded trail, mainly because I was still spooked and worried Brian might catch up with us.

No matter what Yvonne said, I was still convinced he must have seen me.

* * *

THE FOLLOWING MORNING, I was in a quandary. I had been thinking all night of a way to persuade Louise to confide in me. I needed her to tell me her secret, but why would she? As far as she was concerned, I was just a nosy local.

Last night I had tossed and turned, thinking about the possibility of testing my newfound magic skills. I wanted to make a truth potion, which I hoped would convince Louise to open up to me.

As the idea bounced around in my head, I knew I wouldn't be able to sleep, so I'd gotten out of bed, looked through the book of spells and then scribbled down one particular spell on a scrap of paper.

I wrote down the ingredients needed for the potion and saw pondweed listed at the top.

Darn. I hated the stuff.

All the other ingredients were very easy to come by, and pondweed was easy enough to find, too. Grandma Grant kept a large pond at the front of the house, close to the greenhouse, just for harvesting the slimy weed, but I hated collecting the yucky stuff.

I thought Grandma Grant might still have a stock in her greenhouse that I could borrow. I didn't want to ask her directly because I didn't want to let her know what I was doing, but I was confident she wouldn't mind me using her supplies. After all, she was always nagging me to practice my spells and potions.

I could have asked for her help, but I was worried she would try to persuade me not to try it.

If I went to Grandma Grant and Jess afterward and told them I had used magic to get the truth out of Louise, they would be impressed.

So that was how I found myself early in the morning, sneaking around in Grandma Grant's greenhouse. I didn't feel too bad about not asking. After all, I'd helped to collect most of the ingredients in there.

At the back of the greenhouse, she had an old-fashioned, wooden, apothecary cabinet. Inside, there were small glass jars, each labeled with Grandma Grant's spidery handwriting.

I fished the scrap of paper out of my pocket and looked for the ingredients I needed.

First things first, I thought, reaching for the pot of pondweed. Luckily, it had been dried and wasn't quite as squelchy as fresh pondweed. I used a tiny spatula to remove a small amount and put it into the mug I'd brought with me from the cottage.

Next, I searched the rows of jars, looking for Rosemary, the herb of remembrance.

I found that easily, but the next item was a little harder to locate — crab apple bark dust, needed for clarity.

I scanned the rows of glass jars, but I couldn't see any crab apple bark dust.

It was so annoying. I had set my heart on making this potion. Then out of the corner of my eye, I saw cherry tree bark dust. I reached for it. One type of dust was surely much the same as another.

Would it really make any difference?

I stared down at the glass jar. It just looked like dust to me. I added a little to my mug and secured the lid back on the jar.

A noise from behind startled me, and I whirled around to see Grandma Grant, trying to creep up on me.

"What are you doing?" she asked, trying to see what I held in my hands.

I hid the jar of dust and the mug behind my back, and I knew I look terribly guilty.

"Nothing," I said. "I thought I left my jacket in here the other day. I was just looking for it."

Grandma Grant gave me a skeptical look. "You're a terrible liar, Harper."

She was right. I was.

I decided to come clean…well, sort of.

"I was just practicing my potions. I didn't think you'd mind if I used your ingredients."

Grandma Grant's face crinkled with a smile. "Well, why didn't you say so? Of course, I don't mind. I'm pleased you're practicing your potions."

I let out the breath I'd been holding. That wasn't so hard. Perhaps I should have asked for Grandma Grant's help in the first place, but I'd really wanted to impress her and Jess. I wanted to show them I could be a true witch.

"Right, well, thanks for the ingredients," I said, putting the glass jar of cherry tree bark dust back on the shelf. "I'd better be off. I'll see you later."

As I passed Grandma Grant, clutching my mug of ingredients, she said, "Harper?"

I turned and looked over my shoulder. "Yes?"

Grandma Grant studied me carefully and then said, "You will come to me if you need help, won't you?"

I nodded and smiled, but I was determined to do this alone.

I left Grandma Grant's greenhouse and headed for the small trail that traveled between the Grant house and our cottage, considering how I would be able to apply the potion and the spell to Louise.

My options were pretty narrow. I could either anoint her with the potion or get her to drink it. I was sure Louise would wonder what I was doing if I tried to anoint her. No doubt, she would tell me to get the hell away from her before I even had a chance to cast the spell. My best chance would be to try and get her to drink it.

But before I did that I had to try and find the words for the spell. Although important words that had to be included were listed in the book, I could use them in any order. I'm sure some people loved making up their own spells, but I found it very frustrating.

Jess said each spell had to be personal to every witch. But I didn't understand why they couldn't just make it simple? Surely someone could make up a boilerplate template. That would certainly make my life easier.

I got back to the cottage, pulled out the book of spells and scribbled down some lines, making it up as I went along. When I finally had something I was happy with, I checked my watch.

I was ready. It was time to go and see Louise.

CHAPTER 21

When I got to The Oceanview Guesthouse, Louise was sitting on the terrace, watching the boats in the harbor as she sipped her morning coffee.

I discreetly patted my pocket to make sure the potion I'd mixed up earlier was still there. I decanted it into a small vial. That was the easy part. Now, I had to find some way of administering it to Louise without causing her to freak out.

I took a deep breath and walked forward, plastering a cheerful smile on my face.

"Hello, it's a beautiful day," I said to Louise and then looked out over the harbor as the sun glistened on the surface of the deep blue water.

Louise straightened in her seat and blinked as though she was surprised to see me. She seemed to be lost in her thoughts as I approached, and I didn't think she heard me coming.

She gave me a half smile and muttered, "Good morning."

Louise wasn't the friendliest of people, and it didn't look like she was going to make this easy for me. I don't think she meant to be cold. She was used to living in a big city and wasn't used to the friendliness of a small town.

"How are things?" I asked. "I hope you and Carol are doing okay. Is there any news on when you'll be able to go home?"

That seemed to be the wrong thing to say.

Louise scowled and shook her head. "No. That ridiculous man, Chief Wickham, insists we stay in Abbott Cove. I'm getting fed up. I don't have time to hang around here. I have things to do. I need to try and find another job, for one thing. I'm burning through my savings staying here."

I nodded sympathetically. "That must be very difficult."

She hadn't invited me to sit down and join her, so I remained standing beside her table. I could see the half-finished cup of coffee by her elbow, but I could hardly pour the truth potion in that without her noticing.

I was starting to think this had been a very bad idea. Who's to say it would work anyway? Maybe I was better off just asking her about why Brian was blackmailing her.

But then a sudden gust of wind changed my luck. The napkin beside the coffee pot was lifted by the breeze and flew halfway across the terrace.

When Louise got up to retrieve it, I reached for the potion and poured it into her coffee cup.

I'd been intending only to add a few drops, but because I was in such a rush, I poured the entire contents into her cup. Still, that couldn't be helped. In for a penny, in for a pound, as they said in England. Perhaps a higher dose meant the potion would act quicker.

Louise gave me a look as I struggled to shove the little vial back in the pocket of my jeans. I smiled and tried to look innocent, but I'm not sure she fell for it.

She sat back down, placed the napkin on the table and reached for her cup of coffee. I held my breath as she took a sip. She didn't react or pull a face, so I didn't think the potion could have made the coffee taste too bad.

Louise blinked up at me, and I knew she was wondering why I was still hanging around, unwanted and making a nuisance of myself.

This would be so much easier if only Louise was a little friendlier.

"How is Carol getting on?" I asked, determined to stick around until the potion had worked. "It must be so very hard for her to come to terms with Yvonne's death. I hear they were very close."

"You can ask her yourself," Louise said pointedly, nodding over my shoulder.

I turned around to see Carol walking up the steps towards the terrace.

Her shoulders were slumped, and she did look thoroughly miserable.

I raised a hand and called out, "Hello."

She turned when she saw me and blinked. She raised her hand in a half-hearted wave.

It appeared that Carol didn't want to talk to me. She headed straight into the guesthouse, and Louise's gaze followed her.

"She doesn't seem quite with it most of the time. I don't think I've seen her eat a proper meal since it happened," Louise said.

"It must have been an incredibly traumatic experience. Hopefully, when Chief Wickham solves the case, Carol will at least have some closure."

Louise made a little noise in the back of her throat, making it clear she didn't think much of Chief Wickham's investigation.

I wanted to ask her about Brian, but I wasn't sure the truth spell was working yet. I'd given the potion a little while to act, so I guessed now would be the best time to cast the spell. I chanted the spell in my head and then stared at Louise. I couldn't see any change. How was I supposed to know if it had worked?

I supposed the only way was to start asking her questions.

"Do you have any idea who killed Yvonne?" I asked.

There was no point beating around the bush with silly questions. I went straight for the big one.

Louise took another sip of her coffee and then put it down on the table in front of her.

"I don't want to be rude, Harper. And it's very nice of you to be so concerned about Carol and me, but you really need to get out more. You shouldn't dwell on other people's business like this. I know you live in a small town, but it isn't healthy."

Well, that may not have been the answer I was hoping for, but I was pretty sure she was being truthful. She wasn't exactly holding back her opinion.

I decided to take a chance.

"I'm going to be honest with you, Louise. I was walking back from the Lobster Shack when I overheard Brian threatening you last night."

Louise's eyes widened in panic. "What?"

Her skin paled.

I tried to reassure her. "You don't have to worry about me. You can trust me. I only want to help."

Louise shook her head. "How much did you hear?"

"Enough."

I was bluffing. I hadn't heard nearly enough, but would she fall for it?

She seemed indecisive and stared off into the distance as though she were considering her options.

She turned back and narrowed her eyes as she looked at me. "I should have known it would get out sooner or later."

This was it. The spell was working. She was about to tell me the truth.

I leaned forward eagerly.

But then Louise suddenly clamped a hand to her stomach and doubled over, groaning in pain.

"Louise? Louise, what's the matter?"

Louise gave another groan and then got to her feet, rushing past me. "I need the bathroom. I think I must have caught a stomach bug."

I stood there awkwardly for a moment after she dashed off. What was wrong with Louise? Had that been an elaborate ploy to get out of answering my questions, or had the potion made her sick?

Knowing my track record with spells, I figured the second option was more likely.

Could the potion have done some serious damage? I didn't know. I bit down on my lower lip. I'd messed up. I didn't know nearly enough about potions and spells to be messing about with them like this.

There were only two people I could turn to and ask for help. I turned and quickly rushed off, heading back home to find Jess or Grandma Grant.

Jess wasn't at the cottage, so I headed further up the trail towards the Grant house.

When I burst in, Jess was in the kitchen with Grandma Grant, and they were both cradling mugs of chamomile tea.

"I need your help," I burst out.

Grandma Grant looked alarmed. "What's the matter?"

"Don't be angry, I just wanted to try to use a spell on Louise."

Jess chuckled. "What did you try? The Happy Potion? That was kind of you. She must be feeling incredibly down having to stay at the guesthouse for so long."

I shook my head. "No, I wanted Louise to tell me the truth. I wanted to find out what secret she was hiding, so I decided to make the truth potion. I gave it to her by adding it to her coffee and then she just rushed off to the bathroom. I'm worried I may have really messed up. She looked awful."

Grandma Grant frowned. "What did you put in the potion, Harper?"

"Um…" I tried to think. "I used rosemary, pondweed, rosewater, cherry tree bark dust and…"

"Wait a minute," Jess interrupted. "That's not the right ingredients for a truth spell."

"Well, no. I was supposed to use crab apple tree bark dust, but I used the cherry tree bark dust instead. I couldn't find the crab apple one. I mean, they are both trees, right? I didn't think it would make a big difference."

Grandma Grant groaned and theatrically put a hand to her forehead.

"Harper, they are not the same. You have to follow the ingredients as they are printed. The Witches' Council doesn't produce a list of ingredients like that for the good of their health."

My stomach churned with anxiety. "What have I done? Have I poisoned her? Will she be okay? Can you reverse it?"

Jess gave me a scornful look, which I knew I deserved. "It could have been a lot worse, Harper. You know better than that."

"The potion you gave her will have the same effect as a hefty dose of laxative," Grandma Grant said. "She'll certainly have a good clear out, but she should be as right as rain tomorrow."

I exhaled in relief. Thank goodness. I had really been starting to panic for a minute.

"That doesn't mean you're off the hook," Jess said severely. "It could have been a lot worse."

I nodded. I had seriously messed up.

* * *

I LEFT Grandma Grant's house feeling like an idiot. They'd berated me for at least half an hour, which I thoroughly deserved. I had been a careless idiot, and I was lucky Louise wouldn't suffer any permanent damage.

I should give up trying to master spells because they always ended in disaster for me. I would just have to accept I would never be a real witch.

I let myself back into the cottage and saw Yvonne hovering around in the kitchen.

She took one look at my face and asked, "What's the matter?"

It wasn't fair to hide it from her. I had to own up to my mistakes.

"I had a small issue with a potion I tried to make."

I filled Yvonne in on the details, telling her how Louise had to rush off to the bathroom after drinking my faulty potion.

Yvonne listened quietly, and when I'd finished relating the story, she stared at me and shook her head.

"You could have done some serious damage. That was very reckless."

I was well aware of my stupidity, but I was starting to get irritated with people pointing it out again and again.

"I made a mistake, Yvonne, and I'm sorry. But I wouldn't have had to do it if you had told me what the secret was in the first place."

"You can't blame me for what you've done. I've already told you it's not my secret to tell, but I can assure you it has nothing to do with my murder."

I was angrier with myself than Yvonne, but that didn't stop me taking out my exasperation on her.

"Fine, keep your stupid secrets. I'm done. I'm fed up with trying to help. I always mess everything up. I'm going to go and see Chief Wickham and Deputy McGrady and tell them what I overheard between Brian and Louise. From now on, I'll leave the investigating up to them."

Yvonne rolled her eyes. "Don't be such a drama queen, Harper."

"I'm not a drama queen!" I yelled over my shoulder as I stormed out of the cottage. "I'm just fed up with trying to help and getting absolutely nowhere."

Yvonne didn't follow me, and I was glad. I needed some time on my own to cool off.

Grandma Grant, Jess and Yvonne were right. I knew I was a terrible witch, but I'd experimented on Louise anyway. I was so desperate to impress Grandma Grant and Jess that I'd been reckless and risked Louise's health. It could have ended up so much worse.

I knew they were all disappointed in me, and I was disappointed in me, too.

Feeling very sorry for myself, I slowly walked to the chief's office.

I spoke to Linda Ray, the administration assistant, manning the reception. I was still talking to Linda when Joe McGrady came out of his office, holding a mug of coffee. "Harper? What are you doing here?"

"I'm waiting to see you and the chief. I have something to tell you that might help with the Yvonne Dean murder investigation."

Joe looked at me curiously and said, "Okay, come with me."

I followed him into Chief Wickham's office, where the chief was sitting at his desk, polishing off a chocolate chip cookie.

"Harper," he said, smiling at me. "To what do we owe the pleasure?"

As Chief Wickham and Deputy McGrady listened intently, I filled them in on the conversation I'd overheard between Brian and Louise.

I summarized by saying, "I have no idea why, but Brian is black-mailing Louise."

I then went on to quickly gloss over the section of the story where I'd gone to visit Louise earlier that morning. I didn't think they were going to be too impressed by that part.

I was right. Chief Wickham lost his cheerful smile and looked sternly at me. "You should have come to us straightaway, Harper. You could have gotten yourself into some serious trouble."

I nodded, feeling sorry for myself. He was right. I should have gone to them straightaway.

"I'm sorry. I wanted to try and help Louise and find out the secret she was hiding before I came to talk to you."

"Okay, Harper," Chief Wickham said. "We'll leave it there for now. Thank you for coming by."

I looked up, surprised. "Is that it? Aren't you interested in finding out what secret Louise has been hiding."

Joe McGrady said, "We know Louise's secret, and it's not something you should concern yourself with."

I felt indignant. "You already know the secret?"

Joe McGrady nodded. "We don't think it has any bearing on the investigation, but we are keeping an open mind. Thanks for telling us about the conversation you overheard. I think it's better if you don't approach Louise or Brian from now on, though."

"I was only trying to help," I said.

Chief Wickham nodded. "We know that, Harper. But from now on you can help by staying out of the way."

Ouch. That stung!

Joe McGrady led me and my injured pride out of the office, and on our way past reception, he said, "Why are you so determined to be involved?"

I shook my head. I couldn't answer that question honestly. "I feel responsible."

Joe frowned. "Why?"

I couldn't tell him the real reason, that Yvonne was currently floating around my cottage, and she would remain a ghost until her killer was brought to justice.

I sighed and then said, "I suppose it's because I found her body."

Joe nodded and put a hand on my shoulder. "It's not your responsibility, Harper. We will find the killer. Just try to keep yourself out of trouble."

CHAPTER 22

AFTER I'D LEFT the chief's office, I walked back to the cottage. I was feeling pretty miserable. Not only had I messed up, but it also appeared that everybody knew the truth about the secret Louise was hiding except me.

Well, maybe that was a slight exaggeration.

But I had to admit, curiosity was still niggling away at me, despite the fact I knew I was better off leaving things alone now.

I was still irritated with Yvonne for not confiding in me and didn't want her scolding me again, so I made myself a mug of herbal tea and sat outside on the porch.

The sun was shining down, and it was a beautiful day. It warmed the thick forest surrounding our cottage, and the light hit the green leaves in a way that made them appear to glow.

I listened to the birds singing and rested my chin on my hands.

I was coming to terms with keeping my nose out of the investigation, slowly. It went against my inquisitive nature, but I needed to leave the investigating to the professionals.

I brought out my e-reader and switched it on. Getting lost in a book always helped to take my mind off things. I found it was the best way to forget real life problems.

I was so involved in the book that it was some moments before I realized I wasn't alone. I felt a prickle on my skin and had a strange sense I was being watched.

When I looked up, I saw the small, stray cat, with the white mark beside its nose, standing only a few feet from me. Smudge was back!

I slowly put my e-reader down on the porch beside me. I didn't want to startle the cat.

As the sun shone down on the cat's shiny fur, I thought it looked well cared for, but there was no collar to indicate it belonged to anyone.

I crouched down and held out my hand towards Smudge, being careful not to make any sudden movements.

Its little nose twitched, and it fastened its big green eyes on me before taking a tentative step towards me.

"Hello, you're a pretty little thing. I'm going to call you Smudge if that's all right by you?"

The cat peered up at me with its big green eyes and didn't seem to object to its new name, so Smudge it was.

"Where have you come from?" I asked softly.

The cat didn't look scruffy enough to be a stray.

For the next five minutes, I played a waiting game, slowly getting closer and closer until finally I held out my hand and Smudge rubbed a furry cheek against my fingers.

I grinned. There was something about this cute bundle of fur that cheered me up, and goodness knew I needed cheering up.

I allowed my imagination to run away with me. There was no collar, so perhaps this cat didn't belong to anyone, perhaps Smudge could be my cat.

"Maybe we should get you checked out," I said aloud, wondering if the cat would allow me to take her to the vets. I could see now that Smudge was a female cat. She looked healthy enough, but if she had been living as a feral cat, she could have some health issues that weren't immediately apparent.

Smudge gave a little purr as I scratched behind her ears.

Smudge didn't seem as scared and nervous as she had been the first few times I'd seen her, so I hoped she wouldn't freak out if I did take her to the vets.

After half an hour of stroking and cajoling, I managed to pick Smudge up, and she curled up in my lap as I stroked her soft fur.

There was something relaxing and almost hypnotic about stroking her fur as we both enjoyed the warm afternoon sunshine.

If I was going to take Smudge to the vet, I would need a cat box to transport her in, and I didn't have one of those. Although, I knew Grandma Grant had one for Athena.

The nearest veterinary surgery was in Cherry Town, and it wouldn't take me long to take her in and ask the vet to give her a once-over.

If she wasn't a stray, perhaps the vet would find she'd been microchipped. But I couldn't help hoping she didn't have a chip. I'd grown attached to this little cat already.

Smudge surprised me by being very trusting. I walked to Grandma Grant's, and although she wasn't home, I took the liberty of borrowing the cat box. Athena raised her head and glared at me as I walked past holding it.

"Don't worry, it's not for you this time," I said and left a satisfied Athena curled up on the windowsill in the sunshine.

I called the veterinary surgery, who told me they were happy to fit Smudge in between their other appointments.

I'd expected to have some trouble getting Smudge into the cat box, but she was a perfect angel, hopping in as if she'd been in there one hundred times before.

When I arrived at the vets, the receptionist told me they would see Smudge as soon as possible, but it could be up to an hour before the vet could see her. She gave me some paperwork to fill in, and when I'd finished, I asked her where I should wait.

"You'll be better off waiting at the coffee shop across the street," the receptionist said cheerfully. "The waiting room is busy today, and we have a rather boisterous spaniel in there. Smudge might find it stressful, so I'll take her into one of the appointment rooms until the vet is ready for her."

"Oh, okay."

"Don't worry about your cat. She'll be fine with us," the receptionist added.

I guessed they didn't like owners cluttering up the place, but it felt like quite a wrench to leave poor, trusting Smudge behind, especially when she meowed pitifully as I walked away.

As the receptionist suggested, I headed to the coffee shop across the street, which was called Delish.

There was a young girl serving behind the counter, and I went up to look at the selection of cakes. It had been a hard day, and I needed cheering up.

"What do you recommend?" I asked. "I've had a bad day, and I need something delicious to make me feel better."

The girl smiled and pointed to the double chocolate fudge cake. "That's our most popular cake," she said. "It's very rich, though."

"I'll take a slice of that," I said. "And an extra serving of whipped cream on the side."

The girl's eyes widened. "Oh my, you have had a bad day."

I nodded and ordered a coffee to go with my cake.

I took a seat near the counter and waited for my order, fretting about Smudge. The sunshine streamed through the windows and made me feel sleepy. I reached for the paper menu, just for something to read to pass the time and keep my mind off how Smudge was getting along. I hoped she didn't think I'd betrayed her and left her for good.

I'd just been served my coffee and cake when I looked up and saw someone I recognized walk into the coffee shop.

Brian Constantine.

My heart was in my mouth as I quickly tried to cover my face with the paper menu.

Please, don't look my way. Please, let him be getting a take-out coffee.

But I should have guessed my run of bad luck was destined to continue. Brian slipped into a booth by the window and ordered a coffee and a brownie.

He didn't look gorgeous anymore. He looked terrifying.

How on earth was I going to get out of there without him seeing me?

He pulled out his cell phone from his pocket and was scrolling through something on the screen.

Perhaps whatever was on the cell phone would keep him occupied enough so I could run out without him noticing.

But that wouldn't work. I hadn't paid the check yet, and the commotion that would cause was bound to attract his attention.

I figured my only choice was to try and get the check as quietly as possible and then slip out.

I waved the waitress over and asked for the check in a whisper.

"Sorry, what was that?" she asked loudly.

I sunk lower in my chair. As Brian looked up, I ducked behind the menu again.

The waitress clearly thought I was acting very strangely.

"Can I get the check?" I whispered again, a little louder this time.

She looked down at my untouched slice of chocolate fudge cake and shrugged. "Sure. I'll bring it over."

As much as it pained me to leave the chocolate fudge cake

behind, I didn't have much choice. I'd rather leave the cake than be confronted by Brian Constantine.

The waitress brought the check over, and I quickly fumbled through my purse for enough change to leave a tip, when suddenly my phone buzzed and began to tinkle a familiar tune.

Oh no. Not again! It was a text message from Grandma Grant complete with the "William Tell Overture."

Why hadn't I changed it?

Brian looked over sharply and then recognition dawned on his face.

I shivered. There was no escape now. He clearly recognized me, and thanks to the "William Tell Overture," he realized it was me who'd been eavesdropping on him last night as well.

Still, surely he couldn't do much in a public place. There were other people in the coffee shop…Witnesses. I was safe for now.

I STILL HAD HALF an hour before Smudge would be ready for collection, so all I had to do was sit there and wait it out until Brian left. As soon as he left, I planned to rush over to the vets, pick up Smudge and get home as quickly as possible.

Unfortunately, Brian wasn't prepared to play his role in my carefully thought out plan.

He watched me for a little while and then placed his coffee cup back on the table and stood up, giving me a cool smile as he walked over to my table.

I gulped.

"So it was you."

"What was me?" My voice cracked as I spoke. "I don't know what you're talking about."

I licked my lips nervously and pushed my plate away from me.

He sat down opposite me and said, "I heard your phone. You're that girl from the diner, aren't you?"

I was terrified. I could hardly deny it. How many other people in Abbott Cove had the "William Tell Overture" on their phone?

I decided to try and meet fire with fire. After all, I wasn't the one who was in the wrong here. I may have been eavesdropping, but that wasn't as bad as blackmail.

"I heard you threaten Louise," I said, clenching my fists beneath the table, to stop my hands shaking.

I was determined not to let him see I was scared.

Brian leaned back in his seat and chuckled. "Oh, that."

He didn't seem worried at all, and that annoyed me and worried me in equal measure.

"Chief Wickham is onto you," I said.

I figured it was a good idea to let him know that law enforcement officers were on his trail. If he was thinking of trying to get rid of me, that might put him off.

"Pah, I can't imagine he's going to do much," Brian said scathingly. "You know what these small town cops are like. He probably doesn't know how to do anything more taxing than write out a parking ticket."

I was outraged on the chief's behalf. "I'll have you know that

Chief Wickham apprehended a murderer only a few months ago."

"I bet they handed themselves in," Brian said, sounding bored. "He doesn't strike me as someone with much initiative."

I frowned. "Well, you'd better watch out because he is onto you. I told him everything I overheard last night."

Brian's face darkened with anger. "Oh, you did, did you?"

I nodded and inched back in my chair, trying to get as far away from him as possible.

"If you killed Yvonne, you won't get away with it."

"What are you talking about? Of course, I didn't kill Yvonne."

"Well, you would say that, wouldn't you?"

Brian shook his head. "I know you think you know it all, but I'd be willing to bet you don't even know why I was blackmailing Louise."

It seemed I was the only one in town who didn't know what dirt Brian held over Louise.

"Of course I do," I bluffed.

Brian raised an eyebrow, and I could tell he didn't believe me. "No, you don't. I can tell. You don't have the first idea why I was blackmailing Louise."

"Because you're a nasty man with a twisted moral compass," I said, glaring at him.

Brian scowled. "No, I meant you don't know what information I have on Louise."

I shrugged. "I know you're a blackmailer, and that's enough for me."

"It's not my fault," Brian said defensively. "Louise isn't an angel, and money has been short since Yvonne double-crossed me and booted me out of the business."

I waited for a beat and then asked, "So, what is Louise's secret?"

Brian grinned. "I knew it. You don't know."

"Of course I do," I said. "I just want to double check."

Brian laughed at me but then said, "All right. I'll tell you. She never did pay me off anyway, so I don't see why I should keep her secret. Louise was arrested for fraud five years ago. She was cashing checks from her old boss's business account. You can imagine what would happen if word got out. She would never work in the business sector again. Being able to trust your personal assistant is very important. Yvonne shared her bank and financial details with her."

"Did Louise cheat Yvonne?"

I was starting to think maybe I had gotten it wrong. Maybe Brian wasn't a killer, after all. This certainly gave Louise a very strong motive for getting rid of Yvonne.

But Brian shook his head. "No, this happened before she met Yvonne. Yvonne knew about her criminal record, but she said people deserved a second chance and hired Louise. I disagreed. In my opinion, once a common thief, always a common thief."

I arched an eyebrow. "Sort of like once a common blackmailer, always a blackmailer?"

Brian glared at me, but I ignored him. He didn't seem so scary now.

Yvonne had gone up in my estimation. I thought it was kind of her to take a chance on Louise.

"Well, I bet you don't feel sorry for Louise now that you know the truth, do you?" Brian asked.

Actually, I did. It sounded like Louise was doing her best to put the past behind her and was trying to make an honest living. Unfortunately, people like Brian Constantine were determined to make life difficult for her.

CHAPTER 23

I LEFT Brian at the Delish coffee shop and went across the road to collect Smudge. I was a little early, but I couldn't stand Brian's company any longer. He really was a horrible man.

Despite the fact I was early, I only had to wait a couple of minutes before the vet's assistant came out with Smudge.

"She's fine. We think she's been well taken care of, but we couldn't find any chip." Annabel, the vet's assistant said smiling at me. "We can put the word out locally that you've found a cat, but she can stay with you for now."

That was the best news I'd had all day.

"I'll take her back home, and I'll put some posters up around Abbott Cove so she can be reunited with her owners if they are looking for her," I said, even though I hated the thought of someone coming forward to claim Smudge.

Annabel gave me a few pointers on how to take care of Smudge, but I knew I could handle it as I'd taken care of Athena when Grandma Grant was otherwise occupied.

I left the vet's surgery feeling much happier, and on the way to the car, I quickly typed a text to tell Grandma Grant and Jess that I had a new cat and would bring her over to introduce her to Athena later that evening.

Now I was feeling more positive, I knew there was something I had to do. I owed Louise an apology.

I took Smudge back to our cottage in Abbott Cove and met up with Yvonne, who agreed to come with me to The Oceanview Guesthouse. She was eager to see Carol again and hoped her sister would be coping better than the last time we saw her.

I left Smudge with some food and a promise that I would be back soon and headed down to the harbor.

When Yvonne and I got there, we saw Louise sitting on the terrace of The Oceanview Guesthouse. There was a paperback novel on the table beside her and a half-full glass of iced tea.

As I walked along Main Street, I had been running over the words I could use in my apology, but I still didn't know what to say.

How could I apologize without letting her know I was a witch? It didn't seem possible. Any way I tried to explain it, I would end up outing myself.

I stood there for a moment, indecisive. Perhaps the best thing to do was just to apologize for my constant questioning and ask if she'd recovered from her nasty stomach bug.

Finally, I made up my mind. That was the best course of action. I would apologize, but I wouldn't mention the potion. I climbed the steps up to the terrace and started to walk over to Louise when Carol stepped out of the guesthouse.

"Oh, it's you again," Carol said.

I smiled. "Yes, I wanted to have a word with Louise."

Carol's eyes drifted to where Louise was sitting. "Oh, she's asleep. You'd better not disturb her."

I nodded. "I just wanted to apologize," I said. "But I suppose it can wait. Is she feeling any better?"

"Feeling better?" Carol blinked at me.

"She had an upset stomach this morning."

Carol smiled. "Oh yes, I'd forgotten about that. Her stomach isn't bothering her anymore."

Yvonne hovered by Carol's shoulder, and I was touched by the sad look on her face. I tried to imagine how Carol would feel if she knew that Yvonne was still watching over her.

"I spoke to Brian earlier. I hope he has been some comfort to you," I said. I really wanted to warn Carol to stay away from him. I was quite certain that Brian Constantine only cared about himself. Yvonne had been right on that score.

Carol perked up when I mentioned Brian's name.

"You saw Brian? Where was he?"

"He was in Cherry Town. I saw him in the coffee shop there. Hasn't he been back to see you?"

Carol looked distraught and shook her head. "No, he hasn't been back. This wasn't how it was supposed to be. Yvonne forced

Brian to end our relationship. I thought that now she had gone..."

"That must've been very hard," I said.

Carol nodded and wiped away the tears from her eyes. "Yes, it was. But I understood that Yvonne was just trying to protect me. I miss her. I wish I could talk to her just once more. So she could tell me what to do."

Carol began to cry.

I reached out to take her hand to comfort her, wishing there was something more I could do to make her feel better.

Yvonne was hovering right beside us and reached out to stroke Carol's hair.

"If Yvonne was here now, what would you say to her?" I asked.

"There's no point," Carol sobbed. "She can't hear me."

Yvonne had been quiet up until now, watching her sister sadly, but now she turned to me and begged, "Please, Harper, tell her I am here. Tell her I am right beside her."

I shook my head. I couldn't.

Yvonne's lower lip began to wobble. "Please, just do this one thing for me. I'll never ask you for anything ever again. Look how upset she is... What good is your gift if you can't bring comfort to people?"

I shook my head. This was crazy. How could she ask me to do that?

But Carol was so distraught... maybe it would bring her some comfort.

I sighed. I couldn't believe what I was about to do.

I reached out and put a hand on Carol's shoulder.

"You're probably going to think I'm crazy," I said before taking a deep breath, "but Yvonne is with us right now."

Before I went any further, I wanted to make sure nobody could overhear what I was about to say. If Carol reacted badly, I could always deny everything. But if more than one person heard me admit to seeing ghosts, I could be in trouble. I stepped forward, to make sure Louise really was asleep and wasn't listening.

When I got closer, I realized that Louise wasn't asleep at all.

I gazed at her in horror.

Louise's eyes were wide open and staring blankly at me. Her mid-section was covered with blood, and a knife was buried deep in her stomach.

Louise was dead.

CHAPTER 24

I'M NOT sure how I expected Carol to react — maybe to run to the hills screaming, or maybe to run inside and call for help— but I certainly wasn't expecting her to hit me over the head with the heavy jug that held the iced tea.

I saw the jug flying toward me from the corner of my eye, but I couldn't move fast enough to get out of the way. There was a sickening clunk as it connected with my skull and then everything went black.

When I woke up, to my horror it was late at night, and I was surrounded by water.

I had a killer headache and was horrified to realize I'd lost the ability to move my arms and legs. I panicked and then realized why. I was securely tied to one of the struts supporting the pier.

The tide was coming in.

I was sitting on the seabed, and the water was up to my chest.

I tried to scream, but the rag in my mouth muffled any sound I made.

I tried to turn, but my movements were restricted by the rope.

I managed to crane my neck enough to see I wasn't alone.

Carol stood just behind me, the water almost reaching her knees.

"Oh, you're back with us. I thought you might drown before you woke up. I did give you quite a whack. Sorry about that."

She said the words in such a matter-of-fact way it chilled me to the bone.

I grimaced trying to spit out the rag.

It was then I saw Yvonne was there, too. She was darting around, trying to remonstrate with her sister.

"What are you doing? Carol, you can't do this to Harper. Untie her. Now!"

Unfortunately, Carol was completely oblivious to Yvonne.

I finally managed to push the rag out of my mouth and asked, "Why are you doing this? You don't need to kill me. I won't tell anyone."

Carol laughed cruelly. "I'm not that stupid, Harper. I'm afraid I can't spare you now that you've seen Louise's body."

I had been an idiot. Carol's grief had fooled me. I'd never seriously considered her capable of murdering her own sister.

"Why did you kill Yvonne?" I asked.

"I couldn't take it anymore. My whole life I had allowed her to boss me around, but then Brian came along. He loved me, really loved me. We were supposed to be together, but Yvonne couldn't stand to see us happy. She made Brian leave me. I wasn't going to stand for it…. He was my one chance at happiness. I couldn't let Yvonne ruin that."

"So you killed your sister over a man?"

"He wasn't just a man. He was my one true love."

"Your one true love?" Yvonne laughed. "Oh, please. You have always been a little slow on the uptake, Carol, but I didn't think you were that stupid."

Yvonne wasn't helping. I needed her to help me talk her sister out of this. Somehow I had to persuade her to untie me before the tide came in. Ridiculing her wasn't going to cut it.

"Yvonne loved you, Carol. She didn't do it to make you unhappy. Why don't you untie me and we can talk things through? You'll feel better when you get it all off your chest."

"There's no time for that. Brian will be here soon."

"He's coming here? Have you spoken to him?"

A frown flashed across Carol's face. "I don't need to speak to him. He'll come for me. It's meant to be."

Yvonne's eyes widened, and she looked at me. "She really is bonkers."

"Uh-huh," I said. "Well, I'm pretty sure Brian would want you to untie me, Carol."

Carol tittered. "You're trying to manipulate me. Well, it won't work. You know, I was a little worried when you kept hanging around and asking questions all the time, Harper. I thought you were on to me. But you weren't. You didn't have the first idea."

"Carol, stop this now. Untie these ropes."

Carol shook her head.

I tried another approach. "Yvonne is okay. She is a ghost. She is actually beside you right now."

Carol burst out laughing. Her laugh was high-pitched and tinged with hysteria. "Oh, to think I actually thought I needed to worry about you, Harper. You're just crazy, aren't you? I should have listened to the gossip. Everyone says the Grant family are a sandwich short of a full picnic."

I furiously tried to free my arms from the ropes. Carol had murdered two women and imagined a passionate love affair with a blackmailer, and she had the cheek to call me crazy!

"Yvonne, please, tell me what to say. She's your sister!" I shouted as the water lapped around my shoulders.

Yvonne was wringing her hands. "I don't know what to say. She's lost it. She has never acted like this before."

"You've killed two people already, Carol. Don't make it even worse," I said. "You won't get away with it."

"I don't see why not," Carol said. "I've gotten away with it so far."

Then she turned and started to walk away.

"Wait! Where are you going?"

"I need to go and wait at the guesthouse for Brian. I have to tell him that now Yvonne is out of the way we can be together just like we planned."

She began to walk away again, and I screamed at her. "Wait! Please don't leave me like this!"

Carol turned back, and despite the darkness, I could see a horrifying grimace on her face, and I knew she wasn't going to let me go.

Without answering, Carol crept away. I could see the lights from town, but I was so far away I was sure nobody would hear me. I screamed until I was hoarse anyway.

As the cold water crept up my body, I shivered. "Please, Yvonne, you need to get help."

"I can't! No one can see me, and I can't lift anything. I haven't learned that skill yet."

I turned to face her. "Please, Yvonne. You're my only hope. If you don't help me, I'm going to drown."

Yvonne hovered in front of me, her ghostly form shimmering in the dark and then she nodded.

"All right, Harper. I won't let you down."

When Yvonne left, I was alone in the dark and freezing cold.

Surely Grandma Grant and Jess would realize I was missing soon. I'd told them I would bring Smudge to Grandma Grant's house tonight, so they had to realize something was wrong.

But would anyone get here in time to save me? The tide was rising rapidly, and I squealed with terror as I felt something brush my foot.

Don't panic, I ordered myself. It's only seaweed, that's all. You're going to get out of this. You just have to keep calm.

THE WATER WAS COLD, and I couldn't stop shivering. My lower body felt numb. I didn't know if I was trembling with fear or whether the freezing cold water was stealing all the heat from my body. It was probably a combination of both.

The waterline had already risen to my neck. I lifted my chin to avoid getting a mouthful of briny seawater.

All of a sudden there was a horrendously loud bang.

I tilted my head, and from where I was, I could just see a glow that lit up the night sky.

Someone had set off a flare. Was that a coincidence? Or was it Yvonne trying to attract attention?

I heard a faint meow. That's it, I was now delirious. I was so cold and afraid, I'd begun to imagine things. I looked up, and through the gap in the pier's wooden boards, I could see a small black cat.

Smudge! How on earth had the cat made it down to the pier? Had Smudge followed me from home without me noticing?

My lower lip wobbled as I realized, as nice as it was to see Smudge again, I didn't have much chance of getting out of this with only a cat and a ghost helping me.

The first tear had started to trickle down my cheek when I heard the creak of the boards above me. What was that? Had Carol come back?

All of a sudden, Grandma Grant and Jess's faces appeared upside down above me.

I shook my head, thinking now I really was hallucinating.

"Hang on, Harper. Help is coming," Grandma Grant shouted.

Jess launched herself from the pier, landing with a splash in the water.

Her wet clothes stuck to her body as she reached down to try to untie me.

"How did you find me?" I asked.

"That new cat of yours clearly thinks it's Lassie," Grandma Grant said. She eased herself closer to the edge of the pier so she could look down and see me clearly. "It turned up at the house, and she and Athena started meowing. I'd never heard a noise like it. It was unbearable. I put cotton wool in my ears, but they wouldn't stop and followed me everywhere. Eventually, I got the message they wanted me to follow them, and every time I stopped, they started up that infernal meowing again. I realized something was wrong, so I called Jess, and we both made it down here, following Smudge. I nearly had a heart attack when somebody set off a flare on the harbor wall. I don't suppose that was you, was it?"

I shot Grandma Grant a disbelieving look. "Funnily enough, no. I've been a little tied up."

Jess shook her head beside me. "The knots are too tight." Her teeth chattered as she spoke. "We will have to try and force the rope upwards to give us a little more time. You're going to have to work with me, Harper, okay?"

I nodded as a small wave filled my mouth with seawater. It was a good job they'd arrived when they had. A few more minutes, and it would have been too late.

Between us we managed to move the ropes upwards an inch or two, giving me a little more time.

"Betty, from the Lobster Shack, called the police department after the flare went off. Help will be here in no time. Just hang on, Harper," Grandma Grant said.

Why did she keep saying that? It wasn't as if I was going to stop hanging on.

Just as I tried to reply, I caught another shallow wave straight in my face, and I spluttered out the salty seawater.

Jess's gaze fixed on mine. "Who did this?"

"It was Carol. It was Carol all along. She killed Yvonne and then she murdered Louise. She hit me over the head, and when I woke up, I was tied to the pier."

"Wait... Louise is dead?"

I nodded. "I went to check on Louise after the little incident with the potion earlier. I felt guilty and wanted to see if she was okay. When I got to the guesthouse, I could see her on the terrace, but Carol said she was asleep. She wasn't. She'd been stabbed."

"Where is Carol now?" Jess asked. She was still working away at the knots, but she wasn't having much luck.

"She has gone back to the guesthouse to wait for Brian."

Jess closed her eyes and began to mutter under her breath. I guessed brute force hadn't worked so now she was turning to magic.

The ropes felt a little loser, and I regained the feeling in my hands, but I still couldn't get free.

Grandma Grant joined in the muttering, and the water began to whirlpool around me. I yelped in surprised, but I soon realized what she was doing. The water dipped in the center of the whirlpool around my head — which meant I had more breathing room. The water warmed up a little, too.

"Just a little longer," Jess promised and resumed her muttering.

The ropes were getting looser and looser.

Then we heard a commotion coming from the other end of the pier. I could hear Joe's voice along with Chief Wickham's and Betty's from the Lobster Shack.

There was a large splash as Joe landed beside us in the water.

"Hang on, Harper."

I muttered, "Why does everyone keep telling me to hang on?"

Then I saw the glint of a steel blade in Joe's hand and was struck dumb.

He lowered it through the water, cutting through the rope, and an instant later, I was free.

When I stood up, my legs were so cold and shaky I could barely move. Joe put his arm around me and scooped me up. I flushed with embarrassment as I saw the crowd gathered at the end of the pier. It looked like the whole of Abbott Cove had turned up. How did news spread so quickly?

Yvonne was waiting at the end of the pier, dancing with happiness. She was very pleased with herself. "It was me?" Yvonne said. "I managed to set off the flare! It took me a long time, and I had to concentrate really hard, but I managed it, and Betty came out. When she saw that the flare box was opened, she called the police department."

Tears welled up in my eyes. I had a rule about not talking to ghosts in public, but right now, I was so grateful, I let my rule slide.

"Thank you," I whispered.

"You're welcome," Joe said, thinking I was addressing him.

He set me down when I insisted I was perfectly capable of walking. I was starting to really shiver now. I didn't know whether it was because I was so cold after being in the water for so long or whether it was delayed shock.

Betty wrapped a blanket around my shoulders, and then Grandma Grant hurried me along, prodding me from behind and telling me to get inside the Lobster Shack.

As we walked, Chief Wickham asked me questions about Carol, and I told him she had gone back to The Oceanview Guesthouse.

After shouting out a warning to everyone to stay away from the guesthouse, Chief Wickham and Deputy McGrady ran off to apprehend Carol.

When we all gathered inside the Lobster Shack, I began to feel a little better. It was good to be out of the cold, night air and as I dried off I began to relax. Betty handed me a pile of old clothes and told me I could change out back.

CHAPTER 25

I TOOK the clothes Betty had given me to the small room just off the kitchen so I could strip off my wet jeans and T-shirt in private. The boisterous noise coming from the front of the restaurant sounded like most of Abbott Cove had turned up for a party.

It was only a tiny room and contained a small table and an easy chair that Betty used during her breaks when she was working a shift.

Now I was finally alone after everything that had happened, it hit me how close I had come to drowning. I put a hand on the table and took a couple of deep breaths. It had been a close call.

I felt a little unsteady on my feet as I struggled to pull off my jeans and pulled on the pair of pink yoga pants Betty had lent me. They were a little large because Betty was a plus size lady, but they would do for now. Thanks to the stretchy material they didn't fall down to my ankles.

I reached for the plaid shirt, and I was tugging it on over my head when I noticed somebody standing in the doorway. My heart skipped a beat.

At first, I thought I had to be imagining things.

This could not be happening. It wasn't possible.

I shook my head in disbelief as I stared at Carol in the doorway.

In one hand she held a pistol, and the other was tightly gripping Brian's shoulder. The pistol was pressed tightly against Brian's ribs.

The look of terror on Brian's face told me that this was all too real. I wasn't imagining things.

"You told them I was at the guesthouse," Carol said. "How could you?" She spat the words at me as though I was a traitor who'd let her down.

I couldn't believe it. She had just tried to kill me, and she thought I owed her some kind of loyalty...

"How did you get past Chief Wickham?" I asked her as I made eye contact with Brian, trying to look reassuring and get him to calm down.

I didn't want him making any sudden movements and getting us both killed. I'd managed to avoid death once tonight, and I was determined to do it again.

I pushed my wet hair back from my face. "You may as well give up, Carol. Chief Wickham will soon realize you're not at the guesthouse, and he and Deputy McGrady will come back here and catch you with the gun."

Carol's eyes darted around the room anxiously. She gave Brian a little shove, so he stepped inside, stumbling against the easy chair. Carol then closed the door behind her, so all three of us were shut in the room.

Brian took his chance to get away. He scurried away from her and hid behind me.

There was nothing like a strong man in a crisis, and Brian was nothing like a strong man.

Carol raised the gun and pointed it at Brian. "You ungrateful man! I did this all for you. I did it so we could be together."

"She's mad," Brian whispered in my ear. "She killed Louise and Yvonne."

I nodded. "I know. She tried to kill me, too. She left me tied underneath the pier, waiting for the tide to come in."

Brian's eyes widened as he stared at Carol. "What are we going to do?"

"Stop it!" Carol said. "Stop muttering between yourselves. I'm the one with the gun. You should be paying attention to me."

Carol's arms were shaking, and I could tell she was close to the edge. It wouldn't take much for her to pull the trigger.

She swung the gun around to face me. "Get away from him," she ordered.

I did as I was told. I didn't particularly want to be standing next to Brian anyway.

"What are you doing in there, Harper?" Grandma Grant called from outside the door. "Doc Morrison is here. He wants to check you out and make sure there's no permanent damage."

I hesitated for a beat before replying, "I'll be out in just a minute."

I hoped I would be. I could hardly tell Grandma Grant that I wasn't going anywhere right now because Carol had a gun pointed at me.

If I'd told her Carol was here, I had no doubt that Grandma Grant would barge her way in and someone could end up getting shot.

"Don't take too long," Grandma Grant added.

"Okay."

The moment I spoke, Yvonne floated through the door. "Look who I found, Harper," she said and hovered to one side, revealing the ghost of Louise behind her.

I put a hand to my mouth.

Louise looked bewildered as she floated between us.

Of course, neither Carol nor Brian could see the ghosts, so I didn't dare say anything. I nodded in Carol's direction, and Yvonne floated around in a circle and finally noticed her sister was pointing a gun at me.

Yvonne huffed out of breath. "Oh, for goodness sake. And people said I was the drama queen." She turned around and smiled at Louise. "Watch this, Louise. I've been practicing."

And with that, Yvonne reached out and snatched the gun from Carol's hands.

Brian let out a girlish scream as Yvonne carried the gun away from Carol.

Carol and Brian stared at the gun in horror. I'm sure it appeared to float by itself in front of their eyes.

Yvonne turned and grinned at me. "I'm getting quite good at handling objects now, aren't I, Harper?"

I nodded.

The people outside gathered in the Lobster Shack must've heard Brian's scream because the door burst open. Yvonne quickly put the gun down on the small table, but hovered beside it, making sure Carol didn't make a lunge for the weapon.

"Did you see that?" Brian said, looking at me with terrified eyes as he cowered on the floor. "The gun floated!"

As Joe McGrady grabbed hold of Carol and put her in a pair of cuffs, I shook my head. "I don't know what you're talking about, Brian. Have you been drinking?"

It was only a few seconds before Grandma Grant and Jess were both at my side, looking on in horror as Joe led Carol out of the room.

Betty appeared in the doorway. "Are you okay, Harper?"

"Of course, she's okay," Grandma Grant said. "Harper is made of tough stuff."

THE NEXT HALF an hour passed in a blur. Grandma Grant tried to get me out into the main dining area of the Lobster Shack where everyone else had gathered, but I resisted, sticking to the kitchen. I told her I needed a little space right now to get my head straight.

That was only an excuse, though. I really just wanted some time with Yvonne.

Now that Carol had been arrested I thought Yvonne would be moving on pretty soon, and I wanted to be around when it happened.

Yvonne and Louise hovered beside me in the kitchen, and I spoke to them in whispers.

"Did I really deserve that, Harper?" Yvonne asked. "I was killed by my own sister. Was it my fault?"

"I don't think anybody deserves to die like that, Yvonne. I think your sister was a very disturbed individual. She was prepared to kill anyone who stood in her way."

Louise shook her head. "I didn't do anything to Carol. I didn't even suspect she had killed Yvonne. I told her I was going to the police station to report Brian for blackmail. I thought she would be on my side. I didn't have a chance to react before she stuck the knife in my stomach."

"Do you think we'll go now?" Yvonne asked me, looking around nervously. "I don't feel any different."

"I think you'll move on soon. So will Louise. I'm not sure exactly when, though."

Yvonne reached out to hold Louise's hand. "We had a talk, and I apologized to Louise. I'm so sorry about what Carol did to you."

Louise blinked and looked like she might cry. "I'm feeling a little overwhelmed."

I nodded. "It must be scary."

Yvonne smiled. "I'll look out for her. We will help each other through whatever is to come." Yvonne turned to me. "Thank you for trying so hard, Harper."

I shrugged. "I wasn't really much help. I wish I could have done more."

Yvonne shook her head. "You helped me tremendously. I'm sorry that I was such a difficult ghost."

I smiled as I remembered that day in the diner when I'd described Yvonne to my sister as difficult. I discovered that she was much nicer as a ghost than she ever was as a person.

"Now, I can see why you were so determined to get to the bottom of who had killed Yvonne," Louise said shaking her head. "I can't believe it. I thought you were the town gossip. So are you the only one who can see us?"

I nodded. "As far as I know. There are other people who can see ghosts, but I think it's pretty rare. I'm sure I'm the only one in Abbott Cove."

Louise nodded slowly, and I could tell she was struggling to digest the information.

I would have liked to spend longer in the kitchen talking to Yvonne and Louise. But Grandma Grant marched into the kitchen and thrust a mug of steaming hot chocolate in my hand. "Come on, Harper, you have to keep your strength up, and everyone wants to hear your side of the story. Half the town is gathered in the Lobster Shack,"

I took a sip of the hot chocolate she'd given me and then smiled at Louise and Yvonne before following Grandma Grant into the dining area of the Lobster Shack.

People were furiously debating what had happened.

Betty stood up front by the counter and said, "I heard Harper tackled Carol and wrenched the gun out of her hands."

I raised an eyebrow. That wasn't how it happened, but before I could refute Betty's statement, Grandma Grant took center stage.

"Of course, she did. She's a Grant girl," Grandma Grant said proudly, smacking me on the back.

"If she is so smart, how did she manage to get herself tied to the pier?"

Those words came from Graham, Mayor Briggs's chauffeur. He didn't like us much. Grandma Grant had caused him no end of trouble, by lying on the road in front of his vehicle. She wasn't too fond of him either. I was pretty sure he blamed me for losing his job.

Grandma Grant gave him a death glare. "She was smashed over the head with a jug when her back was turned. Even Harper doesn't have eyes in the back of her head."

Betty nodded. "It wasn't very sporting."

I shook my head and looked for my sister. Sporting? We weren't discussing a boxing match governed by the Queensbury rules. There was nothing sporting about it. Carol had just wanted me dead.

The one person I thought would sympathize with my plight was Jess, but she was far too busy talking to the man she'd gone out with a few nights ago, Pete, the one who liked historical re-enactments. I sighed. Even he was here tonight. Was there anyone in Abbott Cove who hadn't turned up?

I was starting to feel a little claustrophobic and took a step back as people began to chant, "Speech...speech!"

Thankfully at that moment, Joe McGrady came back in. "No

speeches," he said gruffly. "I need to make sure Harper is okay. Doc Morrison, have you seen her yet?"

Doc Morrison suddenly emerged from a crowd of people. "Not yet." He walked over to me and led me to a chair in the corner of the room.

He made me sit down and then tilted my chin up so he could look into my eyes and asked me a series of questions.

"How long did you blackout for?"

I shook my head. "I'm not sure. Carol hit me over the head, and when I woke up, it was dark."

Doc Morrison nodded. "I think we should get you to the hospital. It was obviously quite a whack to knock you out for that long."

I groaned.

"Don't be difficult, Harper. You need to go to the hospital," Joe said. "Doctor's orders."

What I really wanted to do was go home and get into my own bed.

"Do I really have to?" I asked Doc Morrison. "I feel much better now."

Doc Morrison nodded his head and looked grave. "It's my professional opinion you should go to the hospital, Harper."

"I'm sure you're enjoying being the local hero, Harper. But I think your adoring audience can wait until tomorrow," Joe said. "Come on. I'll take you to the hospital myself."

I stood up and yawned. I guessed he was right. Hopefully, it wouldn't take long, and I would be back home in bed by midnight.

"This is getting to be quite a habit," Joe McGrady said with a smile.

"What do you mean?"

"I took you to the hospital the last time you got involved in a murder investigation. You really should stop trying to run your own investigations, Harper. It's dangerous to your health."

As far as I was concerned, I never wanted to be involved in another murder investigation as long as I lived.

"What happened to Carol?" I asked.

"She is singing like a canary," Joe said. "She killed her sister because she wanted to be with Brian, who ironically wants absolutely nothing to do with her. It looks like she just snapped. When we get a doctor to look at her, I'm pretty sure they're going to say there are some underlying mental health issues. The Chief is processing the paperwork so I could come and check on you. He's keeping Brian for questioning, too, but now that poor Louise is dead, I'm not sure we will be able to get any of the charges to stick."

As we made our way towards the door, Yvonne yelled at me from outside.

"Harper, quick! It's time. I can feel it happening."

I rushed towards the door so quickly, Joe said, "Hey, what's the rush?"

I didn't reply. I needed to get outside.

As I stepped out into the cool night air, I could see both Yvonne and Louise starting to shimmer. Their ghostly forms turned into luminous prisms, reflecting the moonlight, and slowly, piece by piece, they started to float upwards.

Yvonne's voice was faint as she said, "Goodbye, Harper, thank you for everything."

I wanted desperately to say goodbye, but I couldn't because Joe had come outside and was standing beside me.

But I raised my hand anyway and mouthed, "Goodbye."

I stared at the spot where Louise and Yvonne had been until Joe put his hands on my shoulders and pulled me around to face him gently.

"Harper? What's wrong?"

I couldn't speak past the lump in my throat, so I shook my head.

His clear blue eyes stared down into mine, and he asked, "Are you crying?"

I shook my head again and said, "No. My eyes are sore from the salt water, that's all."

Joe nodded grudgingly, as though he didn't believe me, and then pointed towards town. "The cruiser is parked on Main Street. Are you okay to walk?"

I nodded, but before we'd taken two steps, Grandma Grant barged outside with her hands on her hips. "And where do you two think you are going?"

"I'm taking Harper to the hospital," Joe replied. "Doc Morrison says she needs to have a checkup."

"I'm quite capable of taking Harper to the hospital myself, thank you very much," Grandma Grant said briskly, coming over and putting an arm around my shoulders.

"But, Grandma you don't like to drive in the dark. You said the lights are distracting, and you can't see the road signs."

Grandma Grant glared at me with annoyance. "So, I'll get Jess to take us."

Joe stared at us with a puzzled smile on his face and then said, "Fine. As long as Harper gets to the hospital, it doesn't really matter who takes her. I'll get back to the police Station."

"That's right," Grandma said. "You need to get down to the police station and make sure that crazy lady doesn't escape again."

Grandma Grant left me standing there as she bustled back into the Lobster Shack and came out, pulling Jess by the hand.

"We're taking Harper to the hospital," she informed Jess.

Jess's eyes widened with worry. "What's wrong?"

I waved away her concern. "Doc Morrison thinks I need to get a checkup. I feel fine, though."

Jess nodded. "Okay, I'll get the car. I won't be long."

After Jess had rushed off to get the car, I felt Smudge's warm body curling around my ankles and leaned down to pick her up.

"I think I owe you a thank you as well," I said as I stroked her soft fur.

CHAPTER 26

Jᴇss ᴅɪᴅɴ'ᴛ ᴛᴀᴋᴇ long to get the car, and she picked us up outside the Lobster Shack.

I got in the front passenger seat, and Grandma Grant sat in the back. Jess turned the heat on, and I relaxed back into the seat.

Grandma Grant had asked Betty to keep an eye on Smudge while we were gone, and as Jess drove away from the harbor and up along Main Street, I said, "Wasn't it strange how Smudge knew where to find me. If she hadn't come to you and made a nuisance of herself, you might have never known I was at the pier."

"Cats are curious creatures," Grandma Grant said.

I didn't understand how Smudge had managed it, but I was very grateful. I felt very grateful for what Yvonne had done, too. It hadn't been easy for her to set off the flare.

It was the flare that made Betty from the Lobster Shack call

Chief Wickham. If it hadn't been for Yvonne's actions, Smudge's tenacity and Grandma Grant's and Jess's spells, I would have drowned before Joe arrived to cut the ropes.

"So, I guess I was wrong," Jess said. "Your cat wasn't just a stray, Harper. Do you think Smudge picked you out?"

I liked to think so, but I didn't really know how the whole thing worked.

"I guess she did," I replied.

Jess glanced in the rearview mirror. "Tell us how you found Athena, Grandma Grant," Jess said.

"Well, I didn't find her. Athena found me. It was seven years ago, a normal day by anyone's standards. I'd parked up at the grocery store in Cherry Town. I needed to post a letter and went to cross the road, not paying much attention to the traffic as I was on a crossing. Athena appeared from nowhere and let out a yelp, and I was so surprised I stopped walking just as a truck sped through a red light then crashed into a lamppost down the street.

"When I looked back at the spot where Athena had been, I saw she'd disappeared. I didn't think any more of it, other than counting my blessings I wasn't laying in the road, flatter than a pancake.

"I went to the store, loaded the car with my groceries and drove back to Abbott Cove. It wasn't until I opened the trunk, that I saw Athena was sitting beside the grocery bags.

"She gave me quite a shock, but you know Athena, she gracefully exited the trunk, as cool as can be, and walked inside the house, settling by the fireplace as if she'd been there forever."

I smiled. I could picture Athena doing that.

"Are you all right if we park up here and walk across to the Emergency Room?" Jess asked.

I nodded. I felt fine.

I spent the next two hours being poked and prodded by the doctors in the Emergency Room. Well, that wasn't strictly true. I was in the waiting room for an hour and fifty-five minutes of those two hours, watching Grandma Grant sample nearly every snack from the vending machines. The doctor eventually sent me home with orders to return if I was sick or my headache got any worse.

Jess drove us home, and as she pulled out of the parking lot, she said, "I feel quite left out now. I'm the only witch without a cat."

"I'm sure you'll get a cat soon," I murmured, leaning forward in the front seat to turn up the heat.

"Well, Harper has Smudge now, and it's said every true witch has a cat," Grandma Grant began, "but that doesn't mean she can be complacent. You still have to learn your spells, Harper. Don't forget that."

I groaned. "I nearly died tonight, surely that warrants a night off from you nagging me about spells."

"You don't get off that easily, Harper," Grandma Grant said. "I don't believe in excuses, you know me."

I certainly did.

"Did I see you talking to Pete earlier?" I asked, turning to Jess. "Or was I hallucinating?"

Jess looked a little sheepish. "Yes, we've decided to be friends, but..."

I was immediately suspicious. "What do you mean but?"

"It doesn't matter now. I'll tell you when you're feeling better."

I didn't like the sound of that, at all. "I feel fine. Tell me now."

Jess pulled onto the highway and then shot me a quick apologetic glance. "I sort of promised we would go to one of his reenactments."

"*We?* Why do I have to go?" I protested.

"Moral support, and you can't back out. I've already promised him we would go."

I shook my head. My sister was unbelievable.

My family was pushy and bossy, but I wouldn't change them for the world. As Jess turned off the highway and we headed towards Abbott Cove, I smiled. I lived in a quirky town and had an even quirkier family, but I knew when to count my blessings.

I wasn't much of a witch, and I knew Chief Wickham would give me a stern ticking off for going to see Louise when he had told me to stay away, but I could live with that. As long as I had my family by my side, I could face almost anything.

FIRST CHAPTER OF A WITCHY CHRISTMAS

"That man is the least convincing Santa Claus I have ever seen."

Loretta put her hands on her hips and peered into the makeshift grotto I'd put up in one corner of Archie's Diner.

She had a point.

Bernie Crouch had volunteered to fill the role of Santa Claus. Although we couldn't see him as he was covered by the green felt exterior of the grotto, I could hear him singing a rather inappropriate ditty.

I gave a slight nod rather than replying directly to Loretta because the diner was packed. It was full of mothers and children eager to see Santa Claus, and some of the older locals had turned up to gawp at my dismal design skills.

Still, the children seemed happy with it, and I supposed that was the main thing.

I probably should mention why I don't talk to Loretta in public. She is the diner's resident ghost.

My name is Harper Grant, and I'm one in a long line of Grant family witches. I can see Loretta because I am what's known as a ghost seer or communicator. It is one of my witchy abilities. When I say one of... Well, to be honest, it is really my only witchy ability.

I'm pretty much a failure at everything else. Although my grandmother hasn't given up on me yet and is always on my case, nagging me to learn my spells.

Loretta pulled a peculiar face as little Tommy Breton rushed past me and darted right through her. It was one of her pet peeves. I'd walked through Loretta on more than one occasion, and after each episode, I had to apologize profusely before she would talk to me again.

I think Tommy had had too much sugar. He was a little exuberant at the best of times, and today he was running around, hollering at the top of his lungs.

We hadn't expected our Santa's grotto to be quite such a success, and feeling overwhelmed by the crowd, and Tommy Breton in particular, Archie had retreated to the kitchen.

Archie is my boss, and he is a lovely man, but he's not very good at handling unruly children.

I heard a rather loud hiccup from inside the grotto and frowned. I had my suspicions that Bernie Crouch, our resident Santa Claus, had been drinking.

Before I could decide whether or not to have a word with him, Dr. Madeline Clarkson walked up to me and smiled.

She nodded at Tommy Breton. "It looks like somebody could do with a little counseling," she whispered.

I agreed that Tommy certainly needed some help, but I thought the answer was probably a little more straightforward than counseling.

Across the other side of the diner, at a table by the window, Tommy Breton's mother was sitting using her cell phone and completely ignoring her son. I thought that probably had something to do with Tommy's behavior.

Madeline crouched down, caught Tommy by the arm and tried to persuade him to calm down a little bit.

She didn't look like she was getting very far so I thought I'd help.

"If you're not a good boy, Tommy, Santa won't bring you any presents," I warned.

Tommy shot me a scornful look. "My mom gets my presents. There's no such thing as Santa Claus."

He spoke in such a loud voice, I was sure everyone in the diner had heard him. I shot a worried glance around and saw a dozen pairs of eyes glaring at me.

One little girl waiting in line to see Santa Claus burst into tears.

I grabbed Tommy by the hand. "Come over here with me, Tommy. I am sure Archie has some nice coloring books that will keep you amused."

Once I got Tommy settled with the coloring books, which would probably keep him occupied for all of five minutes, I set about trying to clear some of the tables.

It wasn't easy because all the tables were full and people were standing up and chatting as well. Muttering apologies, I squeezed between them.

Thank goodness we weren't serving our usual menu this afternoon. We were only offering tea and coffee along with a selection of muffins and cookies, and Sarah had made some gingerbread men for the children to decorate.

The smell of the gingerbread filled the whole diner, and despite the state of the tables and the considerable amount of work I would have to do to tidy up, I felt a warm glow of happiness.

I loved Christmas.

I'd persuaded Archie to put some colored lights up in the window to add to the festive atmosphere, and although Archie didn't share my excitement over Christmas, he'd agreed.

My sister, Jess, had helped me create the grotto, and we'd roped in Chief Wickham to construct a wooden frame. Then we covered it with green felt and used large rolls of white foam to imitate snow.

Archie had managed to source a Santa Claus outfit, but when our first choice for Santa Claus, Jonas Klondike, had broken his foot, trying to chase a seagull that had deposited something quite unwelcome on his head, we thought we might have to cancel the whole event. It was Christmas Eve, after all.

Jess and I thought Archie should be prepared to dress up and take on the role, but he was surprisingly reluctant. Fortunately, word spread around the town that we were in need of a stand-in, and Bernie Crouch had volunteered his services.

I was starting to think that may have been a bad idea.

The line of children seemed to be getting longer, but no children were coming out of the grotto with presents.

Loretta hovered beside my shoulder. "You're going to have to go in there and find out what's going on," she said. "We'll be here all night at this rate."

I put down the cleaning solution and cloth I'd been using to clean table ten, and told Madeline, who was trying to persuade Tommy Breton to color inside the lines, "I am just going to check on Bernie."

Madeline looked up with a frown. "He is taking rather a long time, isn't he?"

I marched up to the front of the line and ducked my head inside the grotto. Bernie was sprawled on a chair absolutely fast asleep, snoring.

"Bernie! There's a line of children out here waiting to see Santa Claus."

Bernie jolted in his chair, and his eyes flew open. "Sorry, Harper. It's been a very long day. I must've just closed my eyes for a few seconds."

"Well, there's going to be lots of disappointed children if we don't hurry things along."

"Right. Send the next one in."

I lifted the piece of felt that flapped down over the entrance to allow the first child in line to enter and then walked back to the table where Madeline was sitting with Tommy Breton.

"I can't believe it. He was actually asleep."

Madeline raised an eyebrow. "Oh dear, that's not good news. He has been doing so well."

Although I should've been working, I couldn't help slipping down into the chair opposite Madeline and asking, "What do you mean?"

"Well, you know I don't talk about clients, but it is common knowledge that Bernie used to have a drinking problem. I have been helping him, and he's been doing ever so well, but it sounds like he may have had a relapse."

I nodded. That wasn't good news.

Poor Bernie. I hoped he could see this through otherwise there would be a lot of very unhappy children.

Madeline Clarkson had arrived in Abbott Cove just after Jess and I moved to the town to be closer to Grandma Grant. She was what Grandma Grant referred to as a head doctor. She was a clinical psychologist and offered counseling for a variety of problems. The locals had been a little reluctant to embrace her at first, but she'd been patient and kind with them and eventually she'd been accepted into the community.

Sarah came out of the kitchen holding a tray of gingerbread men ready for the children to decorate. Some of the designs they had come up with so far were interesting, to say the least.

I thought Tommy might like to decorate a gingerbread man, but I hoped he didn't eat any more sugar. He was excitable enough already.

I took Tommy over to the decorating area, which was two tables pushed together, covered with a Christmas-themed tablecloth. A variety of colored icings, silver sugar baubles, and chocolate sprinkles were set out on the tables.

"I think Santa Claus could be a little tipsy," I whispered to Sarah.

Sarah was a short, stout, practical woman with beautiful red hair that she had to keep tied back in a bun for work. She didn't seem surprised by the fact our Santa Claus was slowly drinking himself into a stupor.

She patted my arm. "I'll take him a cup of coffee. Hopefully, that will keep him awake."

Sarah left me to entertain the children as she went to get Bernie a strong cup of black coffee.

I had leaned down and was trying to tell Tommy to leave some of the chocolate sprinkles for the other children when I heard a high-pitched shriek.

Startled, I looked up, as did everyone else in the diner, to see Sarah hightailing it out of Santa's grotto. Her cheeks were bright pink.

She stormed up to me. "The nerve of that man! He pinched my bottom!"

Leaving me gaping after her, Sarah stalked off to the kitchen. I shot a worried look at Santa's Grotto as another child disappeared inside.

Next to the grotto's entrance, Loretta hovered with her arms folded across her chest. She shook her head at me.

"I think you need to take a look, Harper," she said and then pursed her lips in a disapproving fashion.

Hoping that Tommy Breton couldn't make too much mess while I was gone, I walked across to the grotto and peered inside. Although he tried to hide it by shoving the silver hip flask behind his back, it was clear to see that Bernie Crouch was still drinking.

That was the final straw.

I dropped the green felt covering the entrance and turned around to face the line of children.

"Santa Claus will be taking a short break," I announced to groans from children and their parents.

Apologizing, I rushed off to the kitchen. I needed Archie to have a word with Bernie, man-to-man.

When I entered the kitchen, Archie was already shaking his head as Sarah filled him in.

"We can't have a man like that acting as Santa Claus, Archie," Sarah said. "Those children are going to be scarred for life."

"Well, I think you might be exaggerating, and besides, we will have a riot on our hands if we turn people away."

Archie had a point. It was Christmas Eve and parents were feeling frazzled. Everyone was trying to prepare the perfect Christmas, and none of the parents wanted to tell their little angels they wouldn't be seeing Santa Claus, after all.

"Maybe you should do it, Archie," Sarah said. "You'd make a great Santa."

I have to admit it was a good idea. I'd wanted Archie to play Santa Claus all along, but for some reason, he wasn't keen, and we'd all agreed on Jonas Klondike because he had a huge, bushy, white beard which was perfect for the role.

Archie shook his head. "Oh, no, I don't think so. I've never been very good at acting."

"It's hardly acting, Archie," I said. "You just have to put on a red suit and a fake beard and say, 'ho ho ho,' a lot and then hand each child a present."

"I'm not good with children," Archie whined. "I will tell you what, I'll compromise. I'll go and have a word with Bernie and tell him to get his act together."

Archie began to untie his apron. I supposed it was because he wanted to present a strong image, and wearing an apron with flowers and love hearts printed on it wasn't quite the look he was going for if he wanted to take a firm hand with Bernie Crouch.

"And make sure you tell him to keep his hands to himself," Sarah said, wagging a finger in Archie's direction.

"Yes, I will," Archie muttered as he walked out of the kitchen.

I followed him, but before Archie could talk to Bernie Crouch, he was collared by Tommy Breton, who demanded to know what Archie thought of his gingerbread man.

As Archie made appreciative noises and praised Tommy's artistic streak, the door to the diner opened, and my sister, Jess, walked in. Her cheeks were flushed pink from the cold.

"How is it going?" Jess asked.

She'd already finished up at work a couple of days ago and had been enjoying her time off. Jess worked at the local library, and they closed over the Christmas holiday period.

"Not great," I said.

Before I could fill her in on how our Santa Claus was acting out and getting drunk, Jess said, "Don't be so hard on yourself, Harper. Okay, so it's not the most attractive grotto in the world, but the children seem to like it. I've never seen the diner so busy. I think you must have every child in Abbot Cove crammed in here."

I scowled. "And what exactly is wrong with my grotto? You helped put it together!"

"Nothing, it's fine. Don't be so touchy. I came in to ask you if you've seen Grandma Grant?"

I shook my head. "No, not since this morning. Isn't she at home?"

Jess sighed and shook her head. "No, she went out at lunchtime, saying she had forgotten to get some ingredients for Christmas lunch. She's really starting to worry about this meal. I actually think she might be nervous."

"Nervous? That doesn't sound at all like Grandma Grant."

"I know. That's why I am worried. I think she's anxious about the impending family visit."

I frowned. I hadn't ever seen Grandma Grant nervous about anything. But I suppose it had been a little while since we'd seen my parents and my sister, Lily. They were coming to Abbot Cove this year to spend Christmas with us.

When Jess and I were children, we used to spend every summer here, but since then, Grandma Grant had slowly drifted apart from our father, her son. When Jess and I were growing up, our parents had forbidden Grandma Grant from mentioning the M word. We'd had no idea we were descended from the Grant witches of Abbott Cove.

Our father didn't approve of magic, which had made life rather awkward when Jess and I had discovered our magical abilities after we turned sixteen.

I thought perhaps magic had completely skipped a generation, but Grandma Grant told me she suspected my father had suppressed his magical abilities, and that was why he was so anti-magic. Both my mother and father still refused to talk about magic, and that was the reason why Jess and I had moved away from New York City and settled down in Abbot Cove with Grandma Grant.

It's hard to pretend to be something you're not.

They were supposed to be arriving tomorrow before lunch.

"I am sure she'll be fine," I said.

Grandma Grant was the most formidable person I knew. She didn't suffer fools gladly, and she really didn't care what people thought of her. In fact, she positively encouraged the residents of Abbott Cove to think she was a witch. That didn't exactly sit well with Jess and me because we preferred to blend in and not draw attention to ourselves.

I was about to ask Jess whether she thought Lily might be developing her magical abilities soon. Our younger sister would soon be turning sixteen. I wanted to be able to support her through the transition. Although it was possible that she took after our mother rather than our father and hadn't inherited any witchy genes.

But before I could ask, there was an audible gasp from the people in the diner, and I turned around to see Archie staggering out of the grotto.

His face was white as he stuttered, "Everyone has to leave, now. Please take all the children outside."

"What's up with Archie?" Jess asked.

I shook my head. I had no idea. Perhaps he'd had a falling out with Bernie Crouch.

I left Jess and rushed over to him. "What is it? I've never seen you look so pale."

Archie's eyes were wide as he licked his lips, and then he said, "It is Bernie. He's been stabbed."

A NOTE FROM DANICA BRITTON

Thank you for reading my Harper Grant Series. I hope you enjoyed this book! If you have the time to leave a review, I would be very grateful.

If you would like to be one of the first to find out when my next book is available, you can sign up for my new release email here: Newsletter

For readers who like to read series books in order here is the order of the series so far: 1) A Witchy Business 2) A Witchy Mystery 3) A Witchy Christmas 4) A Witchy Valentine 5) Harper Grant and the Poisoned Pumpkin Pie 6) A Witchy Bakeoff.

http://www.dsbutlerbooks.com/**danicabritton**/

ALSO BY DANICA BRITTON

Harper Grant Cozy Mysteries

A Witchy Business

A Witchy Mystery

A Witchy Christmas

A Witchy Valentine

Harper Grant and the Poisoned Pumpkin Pie

ACKNOWLEDGMENTS

To Nanci, my editor, thanks for always managing to squeeze me in when I finally finish my books!

My thanks, too, to all the people who read the story and gave helpful suggestions.

And last but not least, my thanks to you for reading this book. I hope you enjoyed it.

Printed in Great Britain
by Amazon

87673045R00150